Robert Cole Todd, Space Services

Can one man make a difference?
"All he did was see the obvious!"
"That's all any genius ever did."

Table of Contents

About the author

CD Moulton has traveled extensively over much of the world both in the music business, where he was a rock guitarist, songwriter, and arranger, and in an import/export business. He has been everything from a bar owner to auto salvage (junkyard) manager, longshoreman to high steel worker, orchid grower to landscaper, tropical fish farmer to commercial fisherman. He started writing books in 1983 and has published more than 175 books as of January 1, 2013. His most popular books to date are about research with orchids, though much of his science fiction and fantasy work has proven popular. He wrote the CD Grimes, PI series and the Det. Nick Storie series, among other works.

He now resides in Gualaca, Panamá, where he writes the Clint Faraday mystery series, plays music with friends – and pursues his favorite ways to spend his time: beach bum and roaming the mountain jungles doing botanical research. He has lately become involved in fighting for the rights of the indigenous people, who are among he closest friends, and in fighting the extreme corruption in the courts and police in Panamá.

He offers the free e-book, *Fading Paradise*, that explains what he has been through because of the corruption.

CD is the discoverer of the Chadam Protocol for curing cancer. Facebook page Ambrosia peruviana for cancer.

Robert Cole Todd, student pilot Terran Space Services Academy, Luna Base, looked up through the dome at the blackness of space and felt his own insignificance. The human race had come through many crises and events in its history and, though many billions of them had lived how many had actually made a difference? How many were remembered even ten short years after their death?

Man had done much to his planet. Very little of it was good. He had burned, bombed and fought. He was a prodigious polluter. He had so nearly destroyed his world that only a few years ago most of his planet was covered in water because he had poured his filth into his very air until the heat caused the ice caps to melt. Billions died.

The world was almost back to normal now. The pollution was again building and Todd (Everyone had always used only his last name) wasn't so personally sure he didn't hope that if they do it again it gets every last worthless one of them! If you ask for – nay! Insist upon! – disaster enough times the lowering odds will eventually get you.

Luna Base! The big starships stopped here on their way to explore the galaxy! This was the "jumping off" point to man's expansion into the greater universe. This was the place that first step was taken from and from which many more "first steps" would be taken. If the race could survive its seemingly overlong childhood it was all there to be seen and learned. Luna was the first place man had come when he finally broke the bonds of his own world's gravity and it was the first place all came when they were leaving even the solar system itself. It was the place from which the entire galaxy was to be explored!

Well, a few lightyears of it in this immediate area, anyhow.

What about the Goombridgian Federation? Would there be

war?

Todd felt that war with a world fifteen lightyears away had to be the pinnacle of stupidity, but the military kept crying wolf.

What was a wolf? Where did that expression come from?

Maybe it was a demon or troll or something. A childrens' story from before the inundation. The military do that kind of thing to get money and to be able to tell others what to do. If one examines their story none of it makes any sense.

He wished he'd had the chance to go to Mars on the field trip with some of the others in his class, but he WAS the youngest person ever to ever attend the Space Academy so the staff were watching him extra closely. They were, rightly in his opinion, more interested in educating him in the essential skills and specialized knowledge than in escorting him around the solar system. He could get almost everything they now knew or would later learn from these little trips through the sims (Computer simulations) and the books. More.

His entering grades weren't the highest ever recorded in one sense of the term, but were the highest overall since the famous Mike Cogsworth had caused them to revise their entire entrance process and had then shown them they would also have to devise new tests specifically fitted to the individual entrant – and then they would miss half of the important things.

There were many of those whose knowledge or IQ in specialized fields were far above his own. Navigational TTH mode theory had recently had a new grade record set by a brilliant student only four years older than Todd, a beautiful aloof girl by the name of Natalie Komorov. The highest marks in the fields of electronic/positronic applied sensories and temporal computational sciences was that fellow, Nikolas Markolis, just three years before. That was a record that would stand for some time. Very few top physicists really had

any understanding of abstract fractal planal displacements –
and that was the easy part of the science!

Cogsworth was famous in several ways, most of which had
to do with piloting and exploratory techniques. Todd wanted
to be a Spacer pilot more than anything else in life that he
could even imagine so followed that living legend in every
way he could. He had seen "Old Mike" around a few times –
had even talked with him for a few minutes less than a week
before about his grades and unusual abilities. The words,
"Good job, Son! I'm impressed by your stamina. We Spacers
have to be able to stick to our throws!" had put him in mental
orbit, coming from Old Mike!

Todd had heard the expression before, but looked it up after
hearing the "Old Man" use it. It was a reference to the use of
the TTH moder, which was set to "throw" a ship past space,
not a reference to an old game called craps, as he had heard.

Todd didn't care a flip about being an intrasystem jockey.
There were too many of them already. He wanted to be a real
Spacer! A survey scoutship pilot! He wanted to ride the pod
of one of those new Manta class ships! He wanted to be the
first to find a new intelligent civilization. He wanted to be a
great many other things having to do with space and
exploration.

He wanted to be one tenth the man and the Spacer M'tai had
been – or any of those great pioneers. He wanted to be the
new Gagarin or Sheppard. *Those* names would never be
forgotten!

He wanted to land his *own* "Eagle"!

He wanted to grow up! These dreams were, he knew,
childish and unrealistic, but he would never lose them. It was
part of what made Robert Cole Todd tick. He was bound and
determined that some day his name was going to be in the
history books, even for something less than those wild
dreams. After all, how many people ever were remembered
even a mere ten years after they died?

There really wasn't much that one single person could do.

The deal he was offered to fly supplies to the outpost would save him some time and he knew full well he was the best pilot at academy now of any age. An early commission was in the balance if he took these kinds of thing. That was important, but the most important thing of all was that the commission would be signed by Mike Cogsworth.

Cogsworth had shown what one person could do! If Robert Cole Todd could just be one-third of what Mike Cogsworth was his life would be very much worthwhile.

The air was cold. Cold and dry. The clouds were very high and very thin. They cut the light from the white star, diffusing it so there were no shadows. Searing, blinding light came at him from all directions. The area around the direction of the sun was a glaring ache in the sky.

Todd held his hands above his eyes to try to see something. Anything. This featureless white sand would drive him mad faster than the lack of water.

How in the universe could it be so cold with a star that hot? If he could only find ... something. Something to crawl under to get away from that unceasing white glare. He could pass within a few meters of even a whole lousy mountain – which, fortunately for him, there weren't any of – but couldn't hope to even see it through this glare. He couldn't see anything at all unless he was looking down near his feet and in his own shadow.

"Sunglasses! My kingdom for a pair of cheap sunglasses!" he cried. "And a heavy thermal coat, some water, some shade or any combination of those things.

"How long is the day on this godforsaken place, anyway? I've been walking for, let's see."

He looked at the face of the chronometer. He'd been walking for fourteen and a quarter hours.

"Great! The sun's moved about fifty degrees. It has forty

more to go before it sets. Then I'll really find out what cold is!

"One more thing before you get my kingdom! I want a little silly low-wattage hand-held radio.

"And a parasol.

"Lord! I'm freezing and want something to stop the heat!"

He had followed the beam in to find the outstation on this ridiculous excuse for a planet. He had blown the tube linings on three and four during the process. One and two wouldn't sustain him in atmosphere so he sat it down on the planet, meanwhile discovering that the retros were useless after he was too low to pull back out on the two remaining engines. He had skidded for nine kilometers across the silky sand. The slide hadn't harmed the alloys covering the ship, but a static charge had built to such a degree that the discharge after he finally stopped had deprogrammed the entire ship's computer system as well as blowing the collector batteries. All of them. Even the mini-rechargeables in all the portable equipment. He couldn't even call the base to tell them he was down.

He remembered being in the center of those energy bolts that roared through and from the ship. He was in the best insulated spot aboard, the pilot's chair, but had been shocked senseless. He remembered something about hearing someone screaming and was surprised to discover that it was himself.

He had been forced to calculate that the base was in a certain direction, had wound a little clockwork gyro indicator, then had set out in search of the installation – the only one on the whole planet.

He was averaging about six kilometers per hour in this sand and this gravity, had been on the move for fourteen and a quarter hours. That was about eighty five kilometers.

He should be there any minute! It had to be close!

If he missed it by as little as a quarter of a kilometer he wasn't at all sure he would be able to locate the place in this ungodly glare, but the motion sensors at the dome should locate him without any trouble at that distance.

This was definitely and positively the last time he was ever going to volunteer for anything! This was what you got for trying to impress the big brass (Where did that one come from?)! Afoot on some stupid outpost observation planet where you couldn't see and were freezing to death – while you dehydrated.

"You can call this one your apprentice run," Captain Cogsworth had said. "You seem average bright and it's a simple little thing. Eleven light years out, drop the supplies, pick up the experiment results, then back. Take you maybe three days out, a day there, three back, and I'll sign your grade. That'll mean you can be put directly aboard a survey ship as boatman master. It's a fairly easy way to get a commission, but it's up to you."

He had always been quick in the classes where more than one professor had said he was a natural. He could make it on instinct alone.

Sure! Now he was stranded here by some idiot ship that blew its tubes then deprogrammed itself. Next time he'd go for the commission the hard way. It would be easier.

There was the station. He had been right!

"There he comes!" Cogsworth said gleefully. "I told you he was a natural! He homed in on this station like he had a built-in locator beam!

"I don't understand why he didn't try to radio. That's the only thing that worries me about him. It would seem the logical thing to do."

"We wouldn't have answered anyhow," Ellis replied. "What's the difference?"

"I'm just afraid he figured this for a test and decided to outfox us," Cogsworth explained. "We don't need a hotdog on that team. It's much too important."

"He's at the airlock so you'd better hide," Ellis suggested.

"We'll see if he has any explanations. He didn't use the retros and he didn't radio in. That's two very serious oversights.

"If he'd retroed he'd have been less than four kilometers off instead of who knows how many. I don't think he's one tenth as good as you say he is!"

Cogsworth stepped into the adjacent room and quietly closed the door a few seconds before Todd entered the ready room.

"Who the heck are you?" Ellis snapped at him.

"I'm Robert Todd, here with the supply ship," Todd answered. "Had a spot of trouble coming in so had to make the last eighty five or so kilometers on foot. It seems the ship wasn't safety-checked before I left Luna Port. It burned out two tubes so I had to bring it in on dead stick. Retros weren't worth a diddly damn. About ten percent. Skidded the lousy tin crate a lot of kilometers in this sand.

"I'm extremely happy to report there aren't any large rocks or other solid obstructions in the area."

"What!? The retros didn't work?" Ellis asked. "They were supposed, er, I mean, it's unusual for them not to work even when you get some other failures."

"They were *supposed*?!" Todd yelled. "What the hell is this? Somebody's idea of a test? Who could be that stupid! I could very easily have been killed out there!"

"If you had radioed your position you wouldn't have been in any danger!" Ellis retorted. "You didn't follow regulations! The test is a good one!"

"Well, my brilliant friend," Todd hissed quietly through his teeth. "The static charge built up while I was sliding through all that sand and managed to destroy the radio equipment on the ship while it also deprogrammed the computers, so you're going to have one heck of a time getting that ship out of there! You may have to trace and repair every circuit on it.

"The trouble with you people is you can come up with some very interesting little tests for others, but they reveal a few tons more about you than they do about the testee – like you're not in any least way qualified to design those tests if you don't have control.

"I was prepared to complain about the sloppy repair and maintenance work on Luna Port when I came in here, but now I'm getting mad!

"You idiotic damned fool! You could have killed me and never known what happened! Without the radio you couldn't locate me! What if I hadn't known how to put a springloaded gyro together?

"What's the matter with you?"

"Hold it right there!" Ellis snapped angrily. "I didn't design the test and I didn't ask you to take it! I have no control over Luna Port and their snafus! That's not my job! All I do is grade you after you get here!"

"You're so innocent I could puke!" Todd shouted at him.

"He is," Cogsworth said behind him. "And I don't blame you for getting upset, but we have to work it out. We have to find where things went wrong at Luna Port as well as out here to prevent it happening again.

"The ship was supposed to have two bad tube linings and that was all. The rest was to be in perfect condition. The retros were to be checked and in good working order."

"Well they sure as I'm here weren't!" Todd snapped back. "If I had gotten out of that seat while I was dazed. I would have been fried to a cinder! If you weren't an officer who could have me shot for it I'd knock you on your stupid ass so hard your teeth would be in your socks!"

"I wouldn't blame you if you tried," Cogsworth said. "Before you start swinging bear in mind I have the highest degree that can be given in hand-to-hand combat. We can go a couple of rounds or we can try to find where this went wrong."

"It went wrong on Luna Port," Ellis said. "They `fixed' the linings and *didn't* fix anything else. You'd better find out who's responsible before you try that again!"

Todd went back to the ship with the two officers where they planted a locator beam, then went with Cogsworth back to Luna Port where he saw a real military "old-style" officer go berserk and "break" a whole outfit to the rank of basic private. Though Cogsworth was only a captain he wielded enormous power in the space services solely through the fact he was a "through the ranks" spacehand. It was well-known throughout the services that a Captain SV (Space Veteran rank) was somewhat above a four-star general on any land-based base and it had been upheld many times where actual consideration was for the safety of the space-going services. It was said one must go through all ground ranks before he was considered for anything more than little runs like the one from which Todd had just returned.

Todd was going to be placed aboard a survey run ship immediately. That was what the test was about. Cogsworth had explained the whole thing on the way back to Luna Port. The run was to leave Luna in twenty two days so there was no time to go through the paperwork types of testing. Cogsworth and Ellis had come up with the same sort of test that was used when they started themselves. Todd was the fourth testee and the only one to show any real originality.

"It's not that the others won't be good pilots," Cogsworth explained. "They will. They'll be exactly what we need to fill the slots. Make runs like the one that constituted the test. Safe stuff. Ellis doesn't understand the way you pass the test is if you do something innovative. All the others just came in on a standard emergency retro-augmented path. All by-the-book.

"I think you would have set that thing down right on the pad even without the main tubes. Right?"

"I can think of a couple of ways it can be done, but I was mostly just trying to survive," Todd answered.

"Any of the others would have dropped the two tubes back

in and we'd be looking for little pieces of them spread all over the planet," Cogsworth agreed. "I probably wouldn't have done any better than you did – but I would've thought of the static charge and given it more time. You're lucky there."

"I know. I was dazed or I would have waited," Todd agreed. "I'll automatically wait without thinking from now on. My talent is that these things become instinct after once."

"That's your value," Cogsworth replied dryly. "We're going out together on the ship "Ecstasy" in a few days. You'll be my survey team leader, which means you'll answer to no one outside of the "Ecstasy". You'll be totally responsible for your own actions, S Captain Todd.

"Now that we have the same-sounding rank you can call me Mike and treat me like what I am, a spacer, not an officer. Take R and R. Be ready and aboard for liftoff."

"Captain? But I haven't gone through ranks!" Todd cried.

"Staying alive through that landing impressed your superior officer so I've elevated you to a position I feel is within the needs of the service."

"But you can't elevate me to the same rank as yourself!"

"I didn't say 'Captain SV,' I said 'S Captain.' You'll find I still outrank you about fifty grades.

"Ranks don't mean anything out there except at the officer's club or such – and there isn't any officer's club.

"We aren't very formal. Be ready, Todd. I can't wait to get away from these stinking lousy bureaucrats!"

Todd grinned and promised, "I'll be there, Mike."

That was how Robert Cole Todd began his career in the space services.

Chapter one

Robert Todd, S Captain! And just out of school! Now the real work started. Making a grade the way he did was one thing, but living up to expectations was another thing entirely. Luck could take you so far and no further.

That shouldn't be a problem! One thing was true about Todd's life that wouldn't change. When he set his mind on a thing that thing would be accomplished, sooner or later. Always. Period.

Cogsworth certainly lived up to his glowing reputation. Hard as titanium, but absolutely fair. When it came to the services he put them first, and when the services are first all other things automatically fall into place. The people in the service stuck together to take care of each other and of their equipment. They all really cared, and that meant much more than mere words could ever pretend to say. One was very careful about the ship if he and all his friends would die should anything go wrong. In the services everything revolved around the ship. It wasn't only the center of their world, it was their entire world when they were aboard. Literally.

There was much to learn. He must know every operation in case of an emergency and must know where the answers were if he suddenly found himself in charge. "The Professor" – Sgt. Miho – had drummed unceasingly into them that, while it was necessary to be trained to react in an invariant manner in a given situation it was far more important to know where to quickly find critical information that would surely be needed when the immediate crisis was finally over. She said her job was singularly to teach them how and where to find what must be known, not to teach them each little fact.

"Almost anything – any fact – one will need in life is to be found in the nearest public library," she would lecture. "In the

Space Services those facts are stored several additional ways. Special computers are the first line of research. I will teach you to use the computers.

"The second line, should there ever be a power failure or surge erasure – or any of a thousand other things – is in the written word. Printed material. If you couldn't read both quickly and accurately absorb the information you had read you would never have made it to this point. You would be sitting at a desk or doing something landside.

"It would surprise you how many people who work daily with a computer can't get anything from the machine that someone else hasn't listed recall codes for. Some of these people are even considered experts by their fellow workers.

"Not by me! I consider them to be illiterate!

"Knowing what you need is in the machine's memory banks is useless information unless you can retrieve that information! Any bureaucrat can sit at a keyboard and copy a list. Most machines regularly do that themselves, can directly video/ audio-record, translate, store and work with the written word. The operator is simply filling a chair so his superior can say how many people he has `working' under him.

"If you haven't more intelligence than the machine notice there is a door to my left and one to the rear of the room. Walk out of one of them and keep walking until you are out of sight of this Space Service facility and never return! I will *not* tolerate that kind of stupidity! Get a job with the government! The Space Services is one of the few places where *you*, the people, are expected to think for yourselves. If you mess up here on Terra an order is late or you may have to skip your coffee break to straighten it out.

"There are three hundred and two people – no! Spacers! – on a class four ship. If you mess up there you may have killed them all!

"Each of you here has proven you are capable of what we call `transtemporal calculation and immediate action sequence', or 'ticas' thought. You have each passed some test you didn't know you were taking whereunder you moved and thought in a certain manner without even being aware of it. This means that you have considered carefully your course of action, then you have very purposefully followed it automatically in an emergency situation – and in less time than it takes to say 'ticas'!

"That process is a part of you. It can't be taught. It is the very reason you are in this room, in this facility at this point in time. There is no other way you could have come here. You all probably know of someone in your classes or working with you in your last assignments who had some minor emergency arise where they fell apart or panicked. I am quite sure you can understand why *they* aren't here!

"You also must be somewhat puzzled as to why someone who acted as much as brilliantly in some emergency is *not* here.

"If you look back you will see that they paused, thought about what was needed, then reacted deliberately, doing precisely the right thing.

"That pause is what doomed them. Pausing in TTH mode travel means that lightyears of distance could be forfeit – and a lot of things can happen in a lightyear!

"Very few of you are even aware anything happened to you. You are greatly puzzled as to why no one ever tested *you*! – because you didn't consciously think. Your reaction was automatic and correct. It is a thing that is a part of your individual mind, your real self. It is *you*! *That*, I cannot teach! No one can!

"It is one thing to read and even to be able to repeat what you have read accurately, even at some distance in time. You can all do that or you wouldn't be here.

"It is another thing altogether to be able to read, repeat exactly and understand what you are saying! A digital processing recorder can 'read' an entire set of encyclopedias, correct a million misspellings and repeat every tiniest smudge mark on each page a thousand years later, but it hasn't the foggiest idea of what any of it means! – and it can't say the same thing in different words and sentence constructions and keep the exact same meaning.

"I use the term 'constructions' because one could program the computer to use synonyms wherever possible to get the different words alone and even in the same context. The meaning would be subtly different because the machine doesn't *understand* what it says.

"While each of you can memorize quickly and retain what you memorize I am sure you also know someone in your recent past who has what is called `photographic memory' and have possibly even wondered why they're not here, especially as they're probably the very ones who were most proper in the way they reacted to their emergency.

"It wasn't only the pause that got them, it was the simple fact that their mnemonic talent could remember exactly what the books said about a particular type of emergency and they could follow the instructions as though they were following a map.

"Doesn't that indicate that they could not only remember information, but they could also *use* the information?

"Yes and yes! So long as nothing ever happens that hasn't been covered in the books those people are unbeatable! Unfortunately for them, very few things that happen in deep space have ever been covered in any book. Most of them have never before happened at all! – at least not to Terrans!

"Let me guarantee you that you have each and every one shown that your unique subconscious minds can handle the situation for you. It can correlate what you've learned, look at it from various angles, decide whether it will work or if it won't and come up with a plan that *will* work if the books don't cover whatever is wrong. And – and this is most important – you won't even know you have done it unless it is something that is so spectacular it draws attention to itself – such as having the tubes blow on a scout class ship as you are making landfall while you are in atmosphere and suddenly finding that the retros are also faulty! *That*, you would remember.

"I mention this situation because I have seen the glances our youngest member has been getting.

"This is what S Captain Robert Cole Todd – yes! The star and disc are real! – did! His ship deprogrammed and his electronics, little things like radios and beacons, burned out from static discharge. He was eighty five kilometers from base on an outpost planet without life of its own, a sun that is extreme in visible light emissions, but lacking in longer heat wavelengths, and had no directional, visual, or communications devices that could work. He remembered, subconsciously I am quite sure, the gyro leader in his childhood science set, took a windup clock and a stabilizer gyro from the console, made one with some random bits of wire, calculated precisely where the base must be relative to where he stopped – also subconsciously – and marched for more than fourteen hours to come directly to the base. The glare made the base as much as invisible from more than a few hundred meters and the surface of the planet is deep, fine sand.

"This was a test gone wrong. The retros weren't supposed to malfunction. You're looking at the only person I have ever heard of who told SV Captain Iron Mike Cogsworth he ought to knock him on his stupid ass and has no scars to show for it! He has grade and rank above all of us!

"Cogsworth told me all this himself. It's not rumor.

"Now, as to the proper use of shipboard library computers, one must never forget they will do what is asked, but will volunteer nothing!

"Military smarts!"

Todd had slid as far down in the desk seat as he could and

was more embarrassed than he could ever remember being in his life. The last thing he wanted was to be pointed out as some kind of mental freak. Later in the class he noticed that none of them were staring anymore and became somewhat more comfortable.

After the class Sgt. Miho asked him to remain. They had a cup of coffee while she explained that these were very intelligent people who were naturally curious as to how someone so young was able to come from school directly into the services.

"You must also take into consideration that most of them have worked on planetside jobs for years. Making grade isn't an easy thing – far from it!" she explained. "They've been given the true explanation and they've understood why you're going to be on the ship with them. They don't think you're a freak – they know you have a very rare talent. They aren't jealous. They don't envy you your job. Most of them wouldn't take it if they were offered the opportunity. It takes a very rare and special type of person to want to take the chances you will necessarily take. They aren't psychologically fit for it and they damned well know it.

"On the other hand, I am envious! I wanted nothing more in the universe than to have the chance to do what you will do. I didn't make the grade. It's that simple.

"I'm fortunate in that I have the talent to pass on knowledge so can be here at all. For what you're to do it isn't necessary to have years of ground training. It's something that's either there or that isn't. You're born with it or you're not.

"You're very much like Cogsworth, you know."

"But I'm just going to fly a scout!" Todd cried. "There are nearly a hundred scout pilots in the service!"

"There are only ninety two, including you," she replied. "But! There are sixty two thousand eight hundred fifty plus people employed in the Space Services. That's about fifteen hundredths of one percent, in case it slipped past you."

"There are no more teachers," Todd said. "There are fewer in many specialties. There is only one Cogsworth.

"I'm not so special. I'm a damned good pilot – and I won't ever let that loose! – who has a very fast reaction time. I can catch the dollar bill every time. If you hold out ten pennies in your hand and drop them I'll catch them all. Every time.

"I know that ability's pretty rare. My hand/eye coordination is phenomenal. I should know. I've spent years taking tests.

"I set out to be a scout pilot and I get what I want. That isn't a special talent. My folks always taught me that you get what you work for and the first time you make an excuse, you've lost.

"I would never go so far as to set a goal that's too high to attain. That's unrealistic and self-defeating. I could never be even close to what Cogsworth is and has been to the services. That's only a dream.

"Don't get me wrong. I'll very well try! It's very simply and obviously not a realistic goal."

"If it's not getting too personal, I noticed on your records that your parents are deceased," she said. "They did a fine job or raising you.

"What happened?"

Todd's eyes clouded over for a moment. "They were on Flight Seven Seven Four," he answered simply.

That was an atmospheric ship that had was hit by a private plane six years before, raising a huge public outcry against lax regulation of such small craft. Todd obviously didn't wish to discuss it. 209 people died in that crash.

"They taught me to never underestimate myself, but to not go the other way, either."

Sgt. Miho smiled to herself and raised one eyebrow and sipped her coffee with a very satisfied look on her face.

Robert Cole Todd, S Captain for somewhat less than one month in Terran Space Survey team, looked up at the towering silver needle called "Starship Ecstasy" and felt a lump in his throat. He had been assigned to the "Ecstasy" as a survey ship captain exactly twenty two days ago after the test that went wrong. He had figured out how to overcome the sudden problems and had shown amazing natural instincts. Captain SV Carl Cogsworth had personally given him the rank of S Captain and he was now going to go into space! It was so fast and so unexpected he hadn't had any time to react. He fully expected to go into space and on a survey ship when he signed up for the basic, but had no ideas it could come nearly this fast. Most had to work their way up through the grades and didn't reach this point for many E (for Earth) years.

Twenty two days, which he would spend in intensive studying of the newer type piloting consoles.

He went aboard where Cogsworth met him, showed him where to stow his gear and took him to the "rear door" area to show him his ship. The area was called the "rear door" because one whole side of the ship slid open to allow the survey "Chaser" class ships to exit or enter. It was between the crew quarters and the engines, thus was at the "rear" of the ship. His quarters were immediately above the area and he had direct access. The lower hundred and forty feet of the present ship were a hydrogen/oxygen rocket that would lift the new ship above the Earth to deliver them to Luna Port, from which they would then enter the TTH drive that threw them through hyperspace. (That wasn't really what happened, but it was a joke that all the spacers used. There had been much theorized about "hyperspace" a century ago.)

"This will be your ship," Cogsworth explained. "The way we handle these survey type jobs is that you are solely responsible for this ship and will be its sole pilot. Always remember that you will be in it at any time it's not in this mother (as the "Ecstasy" was called), so you'd better see that it's in perfectly maintained condition in all parts at all times.

You're your own test pilot, in other words. If you modify anything be perfectly sure it'll work because you'll test it personally.

"Once you're outside of the mother ship you answer to no one in the way you proceed. We're still in a learning period on these survey details so we have to not only fly, but to do everything else by the seat of our pants, too. That's why the emergency test on Sandworld was so critical.

"Never let it slip your mind that you can be made to answer for anything you do when you return to the mother – by me.

"Ahh! Here she is!"

It was a mini-Manta class 1! It was the newest, fastest, most powerful type of ship yet invented!

Todd felt tears come to his eyes and the lump was back in his throat. It was absolutely the most magnificent sight he had ever seen. The Mantas weren't off the drawing board yet so far as he had known.

Cogsworth was watching him closely and said, "I know how you feel, Son. I remember when I was given the first Penta Class ship ever to fly."

He knew Cogsworth had flown the first Penta, of course. They learned all that in the university. He had also flown the first DD12 and the first TTH ship and was in all the history books along with the Wrights, Erhart, Bleriot, Gagarin, Shepard, Wong, Hinoshi, Lume, M'tair, Orlov, and M'kest.

He ran his hand lovingly across the bright cool metal of the ship while Cogsworth sat on a crate to wait. He knew Todd wasn't capable of speech at this moment.

Todd was to be in the history books, too! Even if it failed he would be the first to pilot a Manta class ship! If it only fulfilled half of the things it was supposed to promise it would advance space survey five hundred percent!

Cogsworth came to him after about ten minutes and programmed the ship to "take orders" from Todd alone. It was attuned to his retinal pattern, prints and brainwave pulses.

They went back to strap in for the flight to Luna Port. Rocket travel was never pleasant.

The "Ecstasy" was four hundred kilometers above a planet, the second from a G2 type sun at thirty one light years from Sol. This was the second stop for the "Ecstasy" this trip out but was the first that Todd would go to alone. He had gone into the first with S Captain Lopez to discover how much things differed in practice from what was taught in the schools. Lopez had proved to be both envious of Todd and afraid for him. They discussed it on the way in.

"I know Old Mike (Cogsworth) got to fly some new ships and is in the books," Lopez said, "and I'm a bit jealous that you get the chance that I never did.

"On the other hand, I was on Asia trip fourteen when M'tair tested the Tumani drive. I saw him and the "Dart" blown to hell and little pieces.

"I guess if I was good enough I would've been offered the job, but I might have turned it down."

"Turned it *down*? Could you do that?" Todd asked.

"Dios mio!" Lopez exclaimed. "Es cierto! No one can be ordered to fly a tester after M'tair! Didn't they tell you that?"

"I guess Mike knew I would give my teeth, arms and legs for the chance. He knows me better than I know myself," Todd replied.

"You might give more," Lopez said, grinning. "Old Mike knows all of us better than we know ourselves. He's really the cagey old coot!

"Which ships have you surveyed for?"

When he explained he was fresh out of the academy and had only flown one test trip Lopez whistled and said, "Mama mia! You must have really impressed Viejo Mike! What happened?"

Todd explained about the landing on the station planet.

When they returned to the "Ecstasy" they were fast friends.

Now he was strapped into the pilot's chair on the newest mini-Manta class ship he had named "Final Exam" and was about to go into history – one way or another.

As they were in orbit he used a high pressure jet to move the ship from the mother a full five kilometers. He was aware this was as close as was safe should anything go wrong with the TTH drive moder, which could shunt power from one dimensional plane to another and make a hydrogen fusion bomb look like a firecracker (whatever the old expression meant. He had never seen a firecracker and didn't have any idea how you could crack fire.)

He eased the ship around on its RJDD tubes to get the feel of it as he circled the "Ecstasy" at five Kms. He knew every piece of equipment aboard was monitoring him and he wanted time for every assessment to be exact. If something went wrong he didn't want another to have to go through this. No one knew if the new drive was workable. Yet.

When he was sure all instrumentation had been given time to adjust he eased the chair back and engaged the drive.

Nothing happened. He felt a little dizzy, but nothing else happened! He cut the drive and radioed to the "Ecstasy" that the drive didn't engage. He waited for an answer, but got nothing but static, so he turned the "Final Exam" to an angle where he could use light beam instead of radio.

He couldn't find the "Ecstasy". As a matter of fact he found he couldn't find the star, the planet or the system.

This was the point where unthinking panic would have hit the average person like a runaway freight train, but Cogsworth's intuition about Todd proved out. He remained calm as he pulled the computer console into place and activated it.

He had all sensors engaged before feeding in all of Earth's identification information. He waited patiently for the machine to do its job.

he equipment located Earth. That was its job and it did it

well.

He then programmed information about Sirius, another star that should be even easier to find than Sol was. When that was known he located Procyon, drew a trace, figured the angles and knew very closely where he was. He then located the star where the "Ecstasy" was and started to throw the drive back in, then thought better of it.

He reasoned the ship recorded everything that happened to it. The ship "knew" where it had come from, "knew" exactly where the "Ecstasy" was in relation to itself and could figure how to get back better than he could.

He simply ordered the ship to set coordinates for the close vicinity of the "Ecstasy", gave it time to figure, then engaged the drive. They popped back into "N" (Normal) space five Kms from the "Ecstasy".

"I'm coming back aboard," he radioed. "Have Lopez handle the survey. I have to meet with Mike and the science officers about this drive."

"This is Cogsworth," the answer came. "I sent Lopez when you disappeared. I wanted to see if you were aground. Come aboard. We're waiting."

He walked into the conference room as soon as he was aboard and picked up a bulb of hot coffee, then sat at the table. His magnetic clothes made him feel much like he was in a gravity field.

"Where did you go?" Sc. Off. Reems asked.

"Just a bit over two lightyears galactic NE by E," Todd answered. "It seems the drive won't be any use in planetary exploration. It goes faster than the "Ecstasy". I went through the planet down there both ways as near as I can figure it. It must work like the TTH drive or I would be a greasy smear across a few hundred acres down there."

Reems took out all the charts and studied them awhile. He lit his pipe (a habit that was forbidden, but SV Captains made the rules for their ships. Reems had to grow his own tobacco back on Earth, cure it and smuggle it aboard. Everyone knew it was an eventually fatal habit, but Cogsworth maintained it was the sole business of the person who smoked the stuff. The ship strained all the effects from the air.)

"The engines are a modified TTH, but we thought they wouldn't exceed LS. They would prove safe as the repulsor fields wouldn't allow you to strike a surface. I don't know what went wrong. They should have worked perfectly!"

Cogsworth studied the diagrams, shook his head, said, "I don't know much about the drive," and handed them to Todd.

Todd had studied the drive in the university so could see most of what had been done to "Final Exam" and which fittings had been deleted. It all looked as planned to him. He was in the process of handing the papers back to Reems when he suddenly snatched them back and called up a computer and screen. He worked for a few minutes, then grinned at Reems.

"Structure times force equals mass. Mass times force equals weight. Structure at forty five degrees equals planal distortion insertion," he quoted the basic theorem. "Mass times distortion equals degree of interplanal entry and mass times energy equals proportion of displacement.

"The TTH drive works by displacement, which is a function of force distortion on structure.

"You're right about the displacement being less in a less force-utilized engine, but you reduced the engines by one half and the inertial mass of the "Final Exam" by more than ninety four percent, which increased planal distortion an overall forty percent and displacement by, let's see, forty percent times fifty percent, I was going, in reltime (relative time) twenty percent faster than the "Ecstasy" can attain. That's as fast as a ship could go until I flew the "Final Exam" out just now.

"There are two TTH engines aboard my ship, so using one,

I can ... mmm, go half "Ecstasy's" relspeed, or twice the speed of white light in a vacuum near Sol. I would still go through the planet and disappear somewhere.

"This could make it possible to take a mother ship out with four mini-Mantas. The mother would stay in an area of space while the survey ships themselves could go to all the systems in that local area of the galaxy in hours, do their surveys and return. We could survey four planets in the time we now survey one and would save days in the moving from system to system.

"The "Final Exam" figured the way back here by itself so the mother would stop in space between systems and wait for the ships to bring in samples and recorded data. The Ecstasy could survey an average of four point two planetary systems every three days considering moving time and gearing. It would be in service for six months out of the year. That's seven hundred plus planets for our scientists to work on. We find one usable unoccupied planet in every seven systems we explore so that's between a hundred and a hundred twenty five new planets a year. It works for me. We'll have to install an atmospheric drive is all."

Cogsworth yelled, "Didn't I tell you? Wasn't I right? By god, we have the best, most innovative mind in the fleet in this boy! He's a genius!"

"But all he did was see the obvious!" Reems cried.

"That's all any genius ever did," Cogswell retorted.

Chapter two

Maybe there are reasons for all the things that happen and maybe not. Todd rather doubted it. Some things merely happened.

The "Ecstasy" was sitting two lightyears away, Lopez was out in a S Chaser (not sub chaser – survey ship, Chaser class) five or six lightyears out on the "other side" of "Ecstasy" and two other ships were out as well surveying planetary systems. The fleet had pretty well learned to stay away from any planet that had any sort of evolved life. It had been a hard-won fight, but xenopsychologist had been screaming their outrage for years at interfering with the evolutional processes on these new worlds and had finally gotten through to Terra's politicians. It was anything but smart to interfere with an emerging lifeform and it was about time the human race stopped screwing up anything and everything it came in contact with.

It was a point slowly won.

He had surveyed two of the planets in the system – one very hot rock with a mercury atmosphere and mercury lakes. Too bad there wasn't much use for the liquid metal anymore.

The other showed a halogen atmosphere and he had gotten out before he got in. The spectoprobes had saved him. Hydrofluoric acid was a bit hard on the finish of the "Final Exam".

He recorded what he could from orbit and skipped the third planet. It was another rock. The fourth planet had tribal beings so he skipped it, recording an "off limits" for the system.

Some of the military minds and some of the politicians were getting back into contacting some of these races. Todd hoped they would get slapped down hard. The rest of the planets were gas giants so he did a quick cursory survey, then returned to the "Ecstasy" to discover there was a disastrously dangerous problem discovered. Some kind of disease had gotten aboard. The fourteen regular crew were all sick, but they were able to warn Todd off so he stayed on the "Final Exam" while the medoff (Medical officer) made her tests. By the time she found something effective against the plague six of the crew were dead and two were in critical condition. Captain Cogsworth SV was in very bad shape so he turned the ship over to Todd. Todd was of Captain rank as were three others, but Cogsworth felt Todd was best able to handle emergencies – not to mention that Todd didn't have the plague, thus wasn't impaired.

The plague had started in the records' section. As a result the ship now had no recoff (recording officer) at all. They were the first four to die – after S Captain Lloyd.

"It's a good thing the lousy damned SOB died," Cogsworth snarled. "I would've had the asshole jettisoned!"

There were strict rules about decontamination. The likelihood of any organism from a different biosystem interacting with the organisms from Earth was slight, but was there. Lloyd had gotten lax and people had died. "Slight" is not "none."

No one could handle the records so Todd, rather than asking anyone who was so terribly sick and overworked to learn it, had studied the machines and their manuals, then had done the work himself. He didn't allow the "Ecstasy" to go to Sol system until the entire ship and all its parts were decontaminated. If this kind of infection reached Earth it could decimate the population in a short time. If it ever reached Luna or Mars it would reach Earth. Once the entire process was known and the organism, a virus, was known, the ship was microwaved, the people were all given the serum and tested until there was no question the virus was gone they went back to Luna Port.

Todd had transposed all the records and had learned to run

the machinery as well as the regular recoff. He was very able when it came to learning anything that was necessary and he never forgot a thing learned. His problem was that he was mentally lazy so had to be placed in a position of necessity before he would even try.

Once on Luna Port he had to go to Earth to report before the Senate, but refused until Cogsworth was fully recovered.

That was a mistake. In the interim the senate had voted a member of its own to run the Terran Space Survey Fleet Commission, a career bureaucrat/politician named Karel Grimes. He was a squat little balding petty tyrant type with an arrogant insulting manner.

Many years ago the politicians had placed the military under the control of the politicians. It was necessary at the time as the world court had just formed the global government and there were several coup attempts. The space services rapidly grew from the military and the laws were still in place so they were stuck with this.

The saving part was that Todd was an intersystem hero, as was Mike Cogsworth. No one was about to question their professionalism or their care. Had Grimes had his way they would have been demoted at best. Lloyd was given the full blame, but Cogsworth insisted it was as much his fault for not personally seeing to it that any under his command followed the rules exactly. He contended that there was no way any officer could escape responsibility for the actions of those acting under his command. The court disagreed and absolved him of any blame, though he still contended the fact some pre-global governmental leaders were able to pass everything negative that happened under their rule off on some lesser or earlier personage who was there solely for the purpose of being the goat or was no longer there to defend himself excused no one.

The "Ecstasy" again left with a new crew in place where those others had died. Todd was in charge of records until he could break in a new unit, as well as being promoted to S Major. They were soon in an unexplored area and were preparing to leave on their next survey when Cogsworth called Todd into the command bridge.

"It's a new ball game," Cogsworth said. "We have a bunch of politicians who know nothing whatever about what we do or how or why running things. It's gonna be a sad state of affairs for a while, I'm afraid.

"We have to find a way around all this or the space fleet will become useless.

"Todd, I did all I could to keep this from happening! This is disaster to the fleet and to the people of the Sol system! You have to be ready to take full command of this ship. I'm going to resign amid enormous publicity. I have to focus attention of the public on what's happened.

"We're all in trouble! Those stinking politicians will have us in a war in no time. They're already making some loud aggressive noises against the Goombridgians. We've almost always gotten along with them since we met them eight years ago. I know they can seem insufferable at times, but we know they're from a very different culture and have different customs. They think we're as bad as they seem to us. We should know that by now.

"Can you imagine how stupid an interstellar war would be?"

"If you quit, I quit, Mike," Todd replied. "The services need you!"

"No, Todd! The services are through if we can't break the politicians' grip!" Cogsworth exploded. "The stinking lousy politicians can't even run their own offices! How in anyone's imagination can they run the space fleet?"

"It's exceedingly easy to outsmart politicians," Todd answered. "I have to find a way to make them pass laws that will cut their own throats for them.

"Mike, there are elections in three months on Earth. If you aren't in the fleet at the time you can run as at-large senator!

You can work from the inside and stay in the reserves. Your name will take a seat if it's announced on the day of the elections! You can retire from active duty and stay in the services, too! I can then use you to introduce a bill. You can also make a lot of noise every time they try to sneak some of their crooked stuff through. We can stop them right at home."

Cogsworth thought for a minute, then shook his head, thought some more and nodded. "Let's go for it!" he said. "Survey these four systems and we can be back on Luna Port in a month. Let's use their own system against the idiots!"

They stood and shook hands.

"We'll beat them at their own silly game," Todd said. "By the time I return you'll as much as be confirmed in your position. I'll use as much of the time as I can learning how to cope with these petty types on their own ground and with their own crooked methods."

"I'm afraid we'll have to stoop to that, but I see no other way," Cogsworth agreed. "Wish us both good luck! And Godspeed!"

Todd saluted smartly, grinned and was gone.

Todd reported to the "Ecstasy" the following morning with all the papers he felt he would need that weren't on board. They were reduced to digital information on disks. He fully expected the announcement that Iron Mike Cogsworth had opted to retire to the active reserves and that he was now SV Captain Todd and was in command of "Ecstasy".

He was shocked to find the first part of the assumption was correct, but he wasn't elevated in rank and he wasn't to command the ship. Colonel Carl Pwester was to command.

Todd was quick to understand that "Old Mike" had a trick or two of his own up his sleeve and merely smiled to himself. This would give him time to study politics and politicians and to figure a way around the mess the fleet was so near to being drawn into. He would have to survey a system and report on everything there, but would still have many hours of time which could well be spent in thought and research. He must make no mistakes here. Mike was counting on him for more reasons than one. He could think on his feet and he could figure angles no one expected. That was his value to Fleet in a lot of ways.

His age was another factor that would throw them. They would expect him to be naive and easily fooled. They were experienced for some centuries in manipulating "raw teen-agers" into doing exactly what they wanted.

They left Luna Base on schedule and would move close to a point where the various scouts could survey planets from roughly equal distances from the mother ship. That point was fourteen lightyears from Earth. The routine of the ship was such that they came "full relstop" (Non-moving relative to the solar systems they were to survey. The motion of the stars this far out toward the spiral arms of the galaxy already had them moving at more than half a million miles per hour!) and had a meeting of all hands before any scouts left the mother ship. Pwester gave the assignments and addressed Todd as "Major" several times so Todd reminded him that he was S Captain.

"Oh, sorry," Pwester said. "I hereby give promotion to Robert Cole Todd to the rank of S Major in respect for his contributions to the service and because Old Mike said I'd flatly well better if I knew what was good for me."

Those political asses had no right to refuse that one!

"Satisfied, Son?" Todd grinned and snapped a salute. He was to go to the star system designated 14M3-T.04P11-X. The X would then become a number to indicate the number of planets discovered there and would then have a new letter added at the end. "A" for non-usable planets with no lifeforms, "B" for non-usable planets with lifeforms, "C" for usable planets with lifeforms, "D" for non-usable planets with lifeforms and "X" for off limits to further closer exploration due to evidence of any emerging intelligent lifeforms. There was an "M" (medical) classification, but that was for planets such as the one with the virus. It was the same as "X," for all practical purposes. One with an "M" was to be avoided at all costs.

Todd's studies had given him some ideas. He was beginning to formulate a plan that would, hopefully, put the Space Service out of reach of the political hacks and, much more importantly, the military.

The outermost planet was a gas giant so was useless, though its moons showed evidence of having vast amounts of radioactive elements.

The next was also a giant and was ringed. It had several small moons, also radioactive.

What was going on?

Todd brought out the onboard computers to make a spectroscopic examination of the star. It was a very young star for this area of the galaxy where the heavy radioactives were not yet decayed. Probably no sense in looking further for life!

There were eight planets and one would be quite a lot like Earth in a few billion years except that it had two medium-sized moons instead of one large. The planet was condensed properly and could be landed on as the radioactivity was in defined areas. It would be a good place for research. It would be a better place for a military installation. Too many of those morons were fixated on nuclears.

Todd thought for a few minutes, then took the recorders out and reset certain dials, erased the information already on them and made a fast run through all the planets to re-record. This would be a definite "X" system. It would show to be far higher in shortrange radioactives than any ship other than the new scouts could hope to survive. Only he and Cogsworth knew it was possible to tamper with the recorders and they had done this before. No one would ever check again but if they did it could be claimed that something must have happened to the recorders and isn't that strange!

If a system had use only to military it should be kept from the knowledge of the military at all costs according to their philosophy. The last thing the human race needed was another way to wage war!

Todd located a small dust cloud and flew into it for a full relstop to pick up some radioactive particles. That would help convince the people on the ship everything was all right with the recorders.

He flew to the outer limit of the system before he reset the sensors back to standard/record, then returned to the ship where he stood off five kilometers and asked for the robots to come out to decontaminate the ship. There was a special crew of the little robots that could seek out the least bit of dust and remove it. They would take the extremely dangerous material back into the mother ship's labs for complete analysis. It meant a delay of as much as a full day, but that was a small price to pay to keep this system safe from the people who could think only in terms of megatonnage and overkill.

Pwester came onto the com to ask what was the matter.

"I'm as hot as a nova," Todd reported. "You won't believe the readings. I'm sure glad this thing's shielded as well as it is!"

"You read it on the Todd/Cogsworth meter?" Pwester asked – so he knew – but why not? He and Mike Cogsworth were very close and shared philosophies on such things!

"Affirmative, Sir!" Todd said. "That is one dangerous place for the human race to ever go!"

"Then it's a big part of our job to see they never go near the place again," Pwester replied. "Carry on, Major! When you have a decontamination completion go to G three T three point oh one. Lopez is having a major problem there with a classification. Help him out."

"Yessir!" Todd snapped and sat back to do some reading of

the tapes he brought with him.

Maybe he shouldn't have taken on those radioactives directly. If Lopez had an emergency time could be of the utmost importance.

Nobody said emergency. Lopez was shielded, too, so he would have been sent if there was any danger.

He was decontaminated in six hours, then told the ship he was off to aid his fellow scout.

The Manta class ships can sit directly on one another with a passage opened automatically between them. Todd was soon standing beside Lopez and asking what was the holdup?

"I can't quite decide if these are developing intelligence or below that level," Lopez said. "It's a touchy line. If Old Mike were on "Ecstasy" I would put it "X," say it was a developing culture and think nothing of it.

"I don't know what Pwester will put up with."

"Carl thinks pretty much like Mike did," Todd replied. "There are billions of worlds we can use without hurting anything but ourselves. When in doubt, put a big sloppy "X" on it!"

"But the maps won't show that!" Lopez cried. "Madre mia! What if he has to show them the data?"

Todd studied the screen for a moment. "This thing isn't on record, is it?" he asked.

"No. I was waiting for you," Lopez said.

"The guidelines say that any culture who are constructing any major projects is automatic "X,"" Todd said. "See that straight canal there?"

It's just a stream that runs along a straight rock shelf," Lopez argued.

"Come in low from over behind this mountain while you're on full recording," Todd suggested. "You can't tell it's a natural formation from that angle. Put it into the computers and they'll decide it's not possible for a stream to go that far without a meander – ergo, it's not natural.

"Over there on that coast. Take a run directly across those rocks that jut out there and cut the resolution by a hair. The rocks are pure black so they'll appear to be smooth. Call it a pier or a constructed jetty. That makes not one, but two `made' constructions. "X." No argument."

Lopez grinned at Todd and said, "Si, jefe! Esta bien!"

Todd grinned back and went back to the "Final Exam" to survey the innermost planet while Lopez found a couple more features that would look like constructions – from a certain angle. When they returned to the "Ecstasy" Pwester read the report, looked at the pictures, grunted and said it was a dry run trip except for a couple of minor moons with relatively rare elements in an uninhabited system.

"We'll really need them in a few centuries," Pwester remarked, dryly. "Todd, there's another system within range. We have the time so run over and make a report on it, okay?"

Todd took the coordinates and was gone. He could see when he first came into the system that it would be a special one. His inboard instruments detected lots of radio transmissions. Civilization. Did they have space travel?

They were surely not far from it! They had atmospheric flights in dirigible-type craft, great generation plants and what seemed to be electrically operated trains and certain other vehicles. They didn't yet have television he could detect, but he recorded quite a bit of the language, then went back where he said it was definitely "X," but it wouldn't be long before they could contact the people.

The standing rule was that a race could be contacted when they had developed travel outside of their system and not before. It was a constant battle to keep that rule in effect because the politicians and the military minds didn't care a hoot if they ruined a whole world for its people by contacting them too soon. The military seemed to think that anyone else must be subjugated before they had the chance to defend themselves.

Todd had always had a strange strong urge to give some developing culture weapons such as the "F" class beamers (Or since Old Mike had shown him what the military was in any case), then to send every politician and military mind in the Sol system to be wiped out by their own hardware.

"Silly!" he mumbled. "But it would really be poetic justice!"

He returned to the "Ecstasy", gave his report to Pwester, then went back to his studies for the return trip to Earth. Pwester came to his cabin where they talked a bit about what could be done. Todd explained that he'd developed a sort of plan, but he must keep it to himself for the time to protect others. Pwester studied him a moment, then agreed. He soon left Todd to the computers. He found two or three little items to try, but it would have to be by ear. It would have to be dictated by the circum-stances they found on their return.

Lopez came to discuss the planetary systems and they decided to get together on any future missions when there was a way to put a planet off limits.

"Y'know," Lopez said. "It's sort of sad to have to do this stuff. I mean, like it would be a disaster to let those idiots on Earth even know about them.

"Why can't people let other people alone? Why do we have to try to run everybody else's lives for them? What makes those politicians think like they do?"

"I don't know," Todd replied sadly. "I just don't have a clue about how they think! Throughout all our recorded history our politicians, kings or whatever have always tried to get power over everybody else. They've taken some really workable systems such as in Polynesia and completely destroyed them for nothing more than a feeling of power and of ownership of something. It seems if the political structure doesn't make a total shambles of everything they touch, the religions will.

"I guess all we can do is try – and I mean to try!"

Chapter three

The election was over. Todd knew Cogsworth would win the seat. He was a global hero who had brought the space fleet up to its present status as well as *the* pioneer pilot of no less than three different types of ship. Everyone knew his name and what he stood for. He was the man most responsible for the inclusion of now S Major Robert Cole Todd in the survey command of the fleet ship "Ecstasy", which had been Cogsworth's own.

The politicians had made their play and were able to place a petty tinhorn bureaucrat as the head of Fleet. Cogsworth had then "retired" to run for the Terran Control Senate and had taken the seat with the largest majority ever recorded.

That could stop the takeover – or slow it down, at least. "Old Mike" could command more public support for anything he proposed than the rest of the crowd combined. It would be a hard battle and a long one.

Any other man in the fleet would've resigned when Cogsworth did what he did to Todd about the command of the "Ecstasy", but Todd knew "Old Mike" well enough to know there must be a definite ulterior motive so he'd raised an eyebrow and remained silent.

Todd had taken command of the "Ecstasy" when the crew had been decimated by a deadly xenovirus, brought it home to Luna Port One, supported Cogsworth in his bid for the senate and had taken the ship out as its commander in its last flight. Cogsworth had then given the command to Colonel Carl Pwester and reduced Todd back to Survey Ship Leader.

Todd liked Pwester, knew that he was next in line for command and that he was a good military strategist, though there was very little need for military skills anymore in the Solarian Terran Empire. Now these crazy idiot politicians seemed to be heading full-tilt into starting a war with the

Goombridgian Federation. War at eleven lightyears distance was ridiculous, but few politicians have ever been known for intelligence – or even simple good sense.

It would be awhile and "Old Mike" had to be up to something, but was time the enemy or the ally?

The trip was a long one. They surveyed a total of forty star systems and had been away for most of two years. Todd had made some minor improvements in the Chaser ships, then had worked out a better system for data storage and retrieval in the maincomps on the ship. Everyone was ready for a vacation when they reached Luna Port so they were given time for one.

There was a message waiting for Todd. He opened it to find the cryptic message: ***I think you should prosecute a plan for the future of your political aspirations immediately. Time is short - M. C. de Slidinsand.***

Not only was the use of English terrible, he didn't have any political plans whatever and had never heard of any "M. C. de Slidinsand."

He was about to throw the silly message away when he thought the only M. C. he knew was "Old Mike" Cogsworth.

It hit him. His first test as a graduate of the university had ended in his sliding several kilometers through sand on a dreary outpost planet. Mike Cogsworth had been there waiting for him – had, in fact, designed the test, though it had gone wrong then.

"Learn to prosecute politicians. Fast! Mike Cogsworth," was the message.

Learn fast. Very, very fast.

Todd could learn anything if prodded into it. He always had the ability and had used it to become records officer for the last part of the critical trip before last. All the information was in the computer libraries – plus the fact he had seen how those political proceedings worked when the senate had called him as a witness.

He also gathered he was not to attempt to communicate directly with Cogsworth yet. There would have been no need of the coded message otherwise.

He spent six days in intense study until he was sure he could handle anything they threw at him as a special prosecutor. He also learned that the senate was making a bid to take over the fleet entirely.

The next message he received was even more cryptic.

324.12MC-5.21.999.

324.12 Mike Cogsworth? What the devil was this? That didn't make any sense. It looked like a library code.

What was MC if not Mike Cogsworth?

Mike had asked him to study prosecutorial arts. Would it be something to do with law?

Certainly! Law! Military law = military code = MC! Standard code rule 324.12 of the military code as revised 5/21, 1999!

He grabbed the console to punch in the question code.

Article 324.12: At any time that martial law is declared or at any time the military is otherwise placed under control of the state or any political command for any reason a revision of the code must be formulated and implemented within a reasonable time or command reverts to the military. A reasonable time cannot exceed two years. The passing of a crisis will represent the bounds of reasonable time.

This was gobbledegook! – Or was it? In less than a week from now the appointment of the present commander would pass the two year mark – and he wasn't, by any stretch of the imagination, a military commander. He wasn't a military anything. He was a petty bureaucrat.

Did "Old Mike" want him to challenge the appointment in front of the senate?

Stupid question! Of course he did!

Todd picked up a pad and began drafting a legal opinion.

It had failed dismally. The senate had passed a ruling to the courts that the code was obsolete and not binding as the space services were not military anymore. They were now purely scientific expeditions.

"Old Mike" had grinned into his hand and winked at Todd.

What was going on here? Did Cogsworth want to destroy the services? What would be gained by all this? Now Mike was signaling for him to do something! What?

He had it!

He stood and was immediately given the floor. These senators were waiting for him say or do something they could then use to discredit him.

Well, he knew what Mike was up to – he thought.

"Your honors," he announced. "I concur exactly with your decision as presented to the courts and as passed by them in unanimous vote."

The senators were looking vastly puzzled and shocked.

"I will give priority orders for all Space Service ships to immediately remove all armaments and to carry scientific logos. The military, by your actions here today, is officially disbanded and those drafted into service will be returned to their home bases. They can be discharged according to established procedures and all purely military installations will be permanently closed as of midnight Greenwich Mean Earth Time tonight. Six hours and twenty four minutes from now.

"I applaud your actions wholeheartedly! This move will cut the huge tax burden to the peoples of the Terran Solarian Empire by more than half. Your wise decision is accepted and will be acted upon immediately!

"Thank you. I move for adjournment!"

The noise was deafening! Most of the senators were screaming at each other and at him. The president of the senate was banging his gavel and screaming for order and "Old Mike" was howling with laughter. Todd noted that most

TV cameras were pointed at Cogsworth. He quickly pulled all his papers together, crammed them into his briefcase and stalked from the room amid the tumult.

"They halted the orders to disarm and disband," Mike told him that evening at his hotel. "They have reinstated the whole thing. The people are powerless to stop them now, but they must be very careful for awhile or they'll have a public revolt on their hands that *will* stop them.

"I don't know how to handle this. I had hoped the action would catch them with their pants down and we could close a couple of bases before they could act. It would have reduced the military greatly and the taxpayers would raise too much of a stink if they tried to start it up again. As it is they have to reduce taxes. You pointed out before the entire planet that there's no need of a military.

"I wish there was more we could do. This is nothing better than a shortterm delaying action."

"There's a night session," Todd suggested. "I'll address them. We just might have a lot more than you guess going for us. I think I've found something.

"Be there, Mike, and have Carl with us as a witness. I have a tiny little idea brewing. Their greed is going to smack them in their collective teeth on this one – I hope!"

Cogsworth stared at him for a moment, then nodded and reached for the phone.

They had dinner before going to the chambers where Pwester met them and asked several questions. Todd shook his head and said he wanted this to be on himself alone if it backfired.

When the debate over the military began he stood. The cameras were there so the senate dared not ignore him. He was called to speak.

"Your honors, we are at an impasse of sorts that need not

be," he said. "The very code you have declared obsolete gives us an easy way out. We still have three days to begin a revision of the code according to its own articles.

"May I respectfully suggest we come together and declare the code in effective extension of ten days, the maximum it may be extended?

"I further suggest a board be appointed to propose a new code that is geared to the realities of today. I would further suggest that Senator Cogsworth, who was in the fleet and who has made the greatest contributions to us all be made acting chairman of that committee. I offer my services and those of Colonel Carl Pwester, who I see is in the audience. His presence here in this chamber speaks greatly of his interest in these affairs and I know him to be a loyal and more than competent commander.

"There would, of course, be two non-military members on the panel to ensure balance and fairness to all."

Cogsworth was looking up at him with a questioning expression, Pwester was unprepared for this and showed it, the TV cameras were on him while the senate was murmuring among itself. Todd held up his hands.

"As I see it, you have disbanded the military and the halting of my orders to immediately implement that fact is not a legal order unless the code is in effect. If it is in effect we can revise it. If it is not in effect we *must* disband the military.

"Thank you, ladies and gentlemen. I relinquish the floor."

It got loud and confused, but just before dawn the code was reinstated with a ten day extension. Todd, Pwester and Cogsworth met in the hotel for breakfast.

"What's your plan, Todd?" Pwester asked.

"I've studied prosecutorial law and, as a necessary adjunct, defensive law. I think we can salvage something here," Todd said. "I know how to use words and I know how to slip things past these horses' asses!

"We have a total of twelve days to pass a new code. The old

code was in need of revision. We can give them senate control of the fleet while taking the teeth out of using it as a war machine against Goombridge or anyone else.

"All they want is control so we can get around most of their objections with the language and presentation."

"They'll never let you and me be on that panel," Mike threw in.

"You're a senator," Todd replied. "Let it be known before the vote that you'll start bringing motions the minute they start that crap and will continue to bring them – worded and designed for public consumption – until the ten days are up and they have to disband the military.

"We have them by the short hairs there. They can defeat it, but will have to take over the government in a junta-style coup as a result so will have zero support of the people. That'll result in repression and there'll be a revolt, sooner or later. They'd better take what's offered or they'll end up with nothing whatever – and probably dead on top of it!"

"I'm in!" Pwester cried.

"There's really not a single thing to lose," Cogsworth agreed. "Okay. We'll give it a go. Better we have a few little items than nothing at all. I want to prevent a ridiculously stupid war with the Goombridgians and I'll do whatever's necessary to that end.

"We all need rest. The senate will reconvene in four more hours. I'm sure you'll want to be there and you'll want to be as fresh as possible."

He stood and Pwester went with him to the door.

"I fully hope the erstwhile senators will stay in meetings until the session," Todd said. "I'm going to push hard for immediate action of the commission, as we only have ten days to revise two hundred years of work."

He didn't bother to undress and was fast asleep before he was entirely in the bed. He had learned long ago to catch sleep in the least time and to make it count. He was deeply asleep and awoke at exactly the time he told himself to awaken. It was a talent.

He felt very alert and fully rested as he walked into the senate chambers to find Pwester approaching Cogsworth's seat, where he joined them.

"I've made it pretty plain that I'll filibuster this thing to death," Mike told them. "They've tried for fifty different deals since I got here, but I'm not buying any of it.

"They'll ask for an itinerary whereby we can promise to even possibly accomplish anything in ten days. What do I tell them?"

Todd grinned at him. "You've decided the best way to handle this is to take the old basic code, save whatever's pertinent, throw out what isn't and revise and update those items in between."

Todd put a large box on the desk. "Here are the five copies of the code you asked me to have printed out double-spaced to work on. It will mean intense work, but you feel we can come up with a truly modern and fair blah blah blah yaketty yak."

Cogsworth grinned and said, "You figure which clauses you can run in on them?"

"I have some great ideas," Todd answered. "What will be most important later are a few innocuous things we'll leave in. They aren't important so we simply will read them and agree to leave them alone. It'll save a lot of time and there's no reason to debate every little thing. We'll be several days into it when we come to them so we can lull the idiots into suicide.

"This isn't stuff we can throw at them soon, Mike. We have to leave enough time so they feel safe, then hit them fast and hard where it hurts most. I'm thinking of five to ten years from now. We wouldn't have a chance anytime soon because they'll be waiting for us to spring a trap they fully expect. If it's too soon they can simply plead mistakes in the rapid revision. If time passes and there aren't any challenges they'll feel safe.

"I really do hope my ideas can be used on a certain few who are here today. I also hope we still have our present `commander' when this breaks out."

"I think it will be very hard to avoid it," Pwester agreed. "They've set it up to their advantage. They'll want to hold to the status quo no matter what and they can manipulate Grimes as much as they choose. that's why he's where he is.

"I'm a patient man. I can wait for revenge.

"I don't suppose you'll share your plan?"

"That may be dangerous. No," Todd replied.

"Here come de judge!" Mike said. "Take a seat. We'll know in a few minutes."

It wasn't an easy struggle. Todd had to be contentious on a lot of silly items and to give in on some things, but nothing that was of really critical importance to his plan. They managed to stretch the process to the point there was only one full day before it must be passed or refused – and to refuse would have allowed the military to legally expire. The two senators on the panel made a report that they had gained most of the concessions they had started out to gain so the code was passed unanimously with an added provision that it could be rescinded for cause at any time. Cogsworth insisted that to leave no limit on the clause would leave the fleet in limbo as to where it stood on any issue and proposed that the code be placed on one year's probation, during which time it could be changed as seemed advisable.

One senator said it would take at least seven years. They were able to make a three year clause – two years better than Todd had hoped.

Things gave the appearance they were well set. Pwester and Todd, who was promoted to Colonel in appreciation of his work on the code, went off on an exploratory trip for over a year.

When the Earth armies, navies, etc. were brought in together under the aegis of the Space Services some ranks were kept from each and the whole thing was almost hopeless to understand so the panel had come up with several ranks. Land forces were Private, Lieutenant, S Sergeant, S Officer and S Commander. Space forces were S Sergeant, which was the crossover grade. You must make S Sergeant to enter the Space Fleet. Next grade was Sergeant SV, Captain SV, Major SV, Colonel, Commander and Fleet Admiral, a new rank taken from the old Earthbound navy.

That was one thing they managed to sneak past the senate. An admiral now outranked the Fleet Commander.

Pwester recommended Cogsworth for the first to hold the rank of admiral and public opinion made it mandatory the rank be conferred. He would have to wait for more than three years before he did anything, but that would be all right. They were patient men.

Todd and Pwester returned to the news that Cogsworth had died of a massive coronary. Before he died he had seen the building of a new ship with a new type of drive. It had been christened "The First Attempt" and Todd found he had been promoted to commander and placed in charge of the new ship. It was untested except in its parts. It would be for Todd to test as a ship.

So that was why Cogsworth advanced Pwester to Commander of the "Ecstasy". This ship was already under construction at that time.

Todd tested the ship and made one change. He traded one of the mini Manta class Chasers on it for the "Final Exam", which he had piloted for the entire time he was on the "Ecstasy".

He discovered there were any number of new and better things on "The First Attempt" on its first trip. He was certain the senate didn't know about them. There was, for instance, a sealed message in the maincomp that wouldn't become available to him until the day after the code was off probation and a permanent law.

The First Attempt" was beyond contact with Earth by more than thirty lightyears when that day arrived and he called up the code for the message.

"Todd, I will be dead and gone long before you hear this.

"I have prepared this ship and know it still must contain many secrets when you read this. You will eventually learn them all, I am sure.

"I am in perfect health and will live for more than twenty more years barring accident or murder. I tell you this because I fully expect to have that happen. One attempt has already been made. Grimes has discovered that I technically outrank him and he wants to ensure that I don't do anything.

"I'm very glad we made the provision that only a Space Fleet officer can work up to the rank and that he must have been in command of a ship in space.

"Do not retaliate for my murder until you can do it for the good of the entire fleet. I know you are capable of being a very patient and exacting person and that little escapes you.

"I wish you well, my friend. I die for the Fleet and I go willingly in the knowledge I have left it in good hands.

"Godspeed."

Todd sat immobile for a long moment, then whispered, "Godspeed, Old Mike. You *will* be avenged. This I swear."

If you've ever been on a spaceship entering TTH drive you've experienced the strange sensation of the "twist" in the mind when the transference disrupts electrical flow in the brain and you know how the senses seem to alter while in interplanal mode.

Todd walked along the walkway to the "lift," which was nothing more nor less than a long tube that went from floor to floor of the huge needle that was "The First Attempt". All outlines were sharpened and light tended toward the green much like the light and outlines one sees before a late afternoon storm. Sounds seem somehow to be displaced and a person talking directly to you is heard as though from a distance. Even the slightest change in pressure or temperature is magnified, as is any touch. There is a slightly brassy taste in the mouth with a contrasting lessening of the ability to smell. It's all scientifically explained as electrical paths being shortened by the difference in dimensional angles that overlap despite the energy shields. Todd was thinking it was rather strange that his own scout flyer was called the "Final Exam" while the mother ship was to be called "The First Attempt".

The first attempt at the final exam?

The final exam of his first attempt?

What a silly thing to think of here! His mentor and closest friend had been murdered in cold blood and he could do nothing – must do nothing – *yet*. That was Old Mike's final request.

But he would do something! Oh yes! It may not be for years, but Old Mike was going to be avenged and the services would be wrested totally away from those bureaucrats and politicians. That was Todd's new and only purpose in life.

Dr. Colonel Ella Forbes, a jolly, slightly overweight (Todd allowed that on his ship if it didn't go too far) and totally brilliant black woman who was chief medical officer stopped him and took his arm.

"You, Commander Todd Sir, are coming with me right now!" she ordered happily. "You're perfectly well aware that each person is to undergo a thorough medical profile before each trip and you never showed up!

"Get in there and disrobe! Now! You are two E-days late!"

Todd started to make a protest he had no time for the examination now.

"As Chief Medical Officer of *The First Attempt* I hereby

relieve you of duty and order that this ship return to Luna Port and that it sits on the pad there until such time as the medical examinations of all ships' personnel are completed!" she said as happily. "You know full well I can make it stick!

"Get the point?"

Todd grinned sheepishly, shook his head and began taking off his uniform.

Ella was also as hard as titanium/chromium/ steel alloy when the situation called for it and she never bluffed. Todd knew she would find nothing wrong as well as she did, but that rule was there for a very good reason. TTH drive was extremely hard on a weak or damaged heart and could be disastrous to any neurological problems. The lesson of the "almost invisibly small" tumor "in an unimportant location on the frontal lobes" of Commander Asaki's brain, "which was benign on top of it" could never be forgotten by any spacer. When he went mad three hundred seven people died in a horrible plunge into a star with Asaki locked in the control cabin.

There was now an outside override control system in two other locations in every ship. No one escaped the medical scans.

"You have a hangnail starting on your left pinkie cuticle, a cute little mole that could turn into a melanoma on your right bun and a blood sugar level that is up two points from last exam. We have to watch that," she said. "Lay on your stomach and I'll cryoexcise the mole.

"Your viral scan is coming in now. You're carrying a rhinovirus.

"See? You could have given everybody aboard a cold! I'll have to microwave your head."

She took a long metal wire with a flat end of a certain size, dipped it into boiling liquid nitrogen, Todd felt the touch of the supercooled rod as a searing burn spot for a split second, then felt the flourouracil salve, then the bandage.

"Don't get seriously romantic for a couple of days unless you want to explain the bandage on your butt!" Ellas suggested. "Get on the MW table and we'll get rid of the cold virus."

The common cold had finally been cured. Certain microwaves of the same type used in cooking could pass through the human body without damaging it, but would cause the chains in the rhinovirus to break, killing the virus. It always gave Todd a headache, but it was take the MW treatment or go into isolation for seven days.

"Okay!" Ella finally said, brightly. "Put your clothes on and get out of here! It's positively indecent! I don't know what I've got, but I've sure got it big! Just about every guy on this ship comes in here and, first thing, they take off their clothes!

"I'm not that kind of girl!

"Well, not usually. Let's say not while I'm on duty.

"Most of the time when I'm on duty. A good part of the time. Never when I'm operating!"

She giggled. "You should see my dirty picture collection!" she said as she took the camera prints out to add to his file.

"You got any good pictures of Carman Arelio in records?" Todd asked, grinning at her.

"I got pictures of everybody here!" she said. "Feelthy peectures in good poses! You buy, sailor? A dollar? I sell a lot of your pictures. People throw darts at them!"

"I get half of the profits!" Todd said.

"Ten percent! Not a penny more!" she cried.

It was no use trying to get the best of her in these games.

He smiled, saluted and went out. She waited until he was a ways down the hall, then stuck her head out the door to yell, "Hey, Commander! Love those little yellow duckies on your shorts! Where'd you get them?"

He felt his face becoming red, but couldn't think of a reply so he sniffed and marched away with his nose in the air.

That woman kept the whole crew sane. She was a psychological "key" who had been chosen as much for her sense of humor and her total lack of inhibitions as for the fact there was no better medical officer in the services. She could defuse a tense situation with an unexpected wisecrack at just the right moment. It was a natural thing with her, not a thing that could be taught in some school.

Todd went to the ship bay where he carefully inspected the tracks for the doors that slid apart from a bubble pod (which was a clear plastic ball with him and air inside). The scouts were attached to the "floor" with tethering cables and with a flexible "tunnel" with air, but there was no air in the bay itself as it was large enough for four ships. The air would be lost every time they opened the side of the ship to let them in and out.

The ball had a cable from the top and from the bottom that attached to a track with a motor to move him around the whole area with the push of several buttons for right, left, up, down, rear and forward.

Small bits of debris on the tracks the doors rode on could jam the huge curved plates and were very difficult to remove with the mass of the doors pinioning against the tracks. The weight of the doors was close to zero in space, but their mass was the same anywhere. One who forgot that action/reaction is based on mass and not weight could be flattened to a grease spot! It made no least difference to the human body if it was hit by a weight of twelve tons moving at fifteen miles per hour or if it was hit by a mass of twelve tons moving at fifteen miles per hour. It was just as dead!

Todd removed a few little pieces that probably wouldn't have made a difference in the operation of the doors – but "probably" wasn't good enough. Someone was going to get a dressing down for not doing their job. They could get one of his pictures from Ella and throw darts at it.

Todd grinned and decided to put out a general warning that the next time he inspected anything whatever that wasn't maintained properly a few butts would be kicked. Hard and publicly!

Everyone knew he was inspecting all he could. He always did. They would get the message and no bad feelings.

He inspected the atmosphere generators, then the power level indicators, then his own scout.

It was to the pilot to constantly monitor and maintain his own ship. The ships were keyed to the pilot so no one else could get in without that pilot setting the security system to permit entry clearance.

Natalie Kormovich was inspecting her ship and they spoke a few minutes about the system they were to explore. She asked how he could remain a pilot, yet be commander, too. He explained that the mother ship wasn't in motion when the scouts were out so needed no commander, so he put somebody like Ella in charge and went out as a scout.

"We make our own rules of command out here in space," he said. "Once a scout, always a scout. Old Mike Cogsworth would sneak aboard my scout at times when he had the "Ecstasy" and so did Pwester, though Carl wasn't really a scout pilot like Mike had been."

"I want to know the rules you'll follow about "X"-ing out planets," she requested. "I hear we are to always "X" a planet if there's any doubt whatever. That seems wasteful."

"There are approximately two billion planets in the area we can reach according to theory and it's held up pretty close to exactly that so far," Todd replied. "Of those two billion a maximum of twenty one percent fall under even the most liberal reading of the rules. That's also checking out very closely to projection.

"That leaves more than one and a half billion planets that don't fit the pattern in any way whatever. When you consider what damage we might do by interfering in those less than a billion planets it would be well to consider where waste ends and greed begins. We could depopulate the Sol system if we put a single person on each planet that can't possibly be "X"-ed off. When considering how to classify a whole world where you could do monstrous damage with a wrong decision perhaps it would be wise if you were to ask yourself your own motives. History will remember you equally for the planets you place in any category. The idea that someone will ever discover a planet with the potential of solving all of our problems or will make life any easier or safer on Earth has been shown to be as much as ridiculous."

"I understand K'lista discovered a planet that has literally hundreds of cubic miles of pure gold gravel that can be dug with shovels!" she said haughtily. "That kind of wealth could end a lot of suffering on Earth."

"How did you ever make scout pilot?" Todd asked dryly. "Scout pilots are supposed to be able to think.

"Tell me, Sgt. Kormovich, what makes gold so valuable? It's a good non-corroding coating for tuners and certain circuitry. What else?"

"It's used to make fine jewelry, which can be converted into working capital, which can be converted into food and medical supplies," she retorted.

"It's valuable for jewelry for only one reason," Todd insisted patiently. "Try as you might to avoid it you WILL tell me why it has value. You might as well say it and get it over with."

Todd could almost see her trying to think of a way out, but she had trapped herself and knew it.

"It's rare," she mumbled. "Rarity is value."

"If emeralds looked like dead roaches would they still be valuable?" Todd asked. "There are other qualities, but rarity is foremost.

"Gold will remain valuable only so long as we leave that lousy gold right the hell where it is. If we take a shipload to Earth, even a standard research carrier, gold will have little value anymore. The twelve tons the R-carrier could bring would destroy world markets overnight. That was decided long ago. That's why the `find' has no practical value or meaning.

"I'm personally quite glad the planet was a heavy metal planet without life.

"You see, one person did get an R-carrier of gold to Earth: K'lista! In one of the extremely rare flashes of intelligence that Earth's politicians have ever been known to show they sent that ship back out and dumped it into the sun. That amount of gold would have ruined the economy of the planet."

"There are other things!" Natalie cried.

"Really?" Todd replied. "Name one! I mean one that finding a really large supply of would be worth destroying an emerging lifeform for."

She glared at him for a minute, then grinned. "Point taken," she said. "I'm new at this and still have my dreams."

"We all do," Todd agreed. "I can tell you of one thing that would be valuable for the good it would do, probably several.

"Phosphorus, which isn't all that valuable, is the element that life must have on Earth and that's in shortest supply, relatively. There are other things not so valuable, monetarily speaking, but of vast importance. You'll learn that those things are out there, but usually on smaller moons and asteroids as planets tend to be more varied and much more homogenous.

"Look at that moon in the Sol system, Io. It's mostly pure sulfur for miles in depth. It's there for the taking. Those kinds of things are the most important and they're virtually never on a planet that can be classified "X" even by the most extreme stretching of a point. Life can't exist in pure sulfur or in pure anything else. There isn't even a wild theory for life existing without a quite complex chemistry and that leaves worlds, moons or asteroids with too high a concentration of one thing out of the running.

"Those are the very worlds we seek. There's really no conflict in the classification system. Only the military would want worlds without logical consideration of the natural processes of the universe and there's less and less room in the galaxy for that kind of mind."

"Your feelings about the military are well-known and I think you've convinced me. I never really stopped to think about all that before, but you're right. Only a homogenous planet could support life and that precludes deposits of anything like that gold." she said. "It's good to know where we stand on some of these things. I will admit I'm not so concerned about some lifeform that may be important a million years or so from now but, as you point out, what's the difference when we have billions of planets where the problem doesn't arise at all?" She saluted and went back into her scout.

Todd hoped she wouldn't see the obvious – that he was far too simplistic. There *would be* planets that didn't fit.

Chapter four

"Commander Todd! Come to communications. Stat!, Commander Todd!" woke him from a restful sleep. He sighed deeply and hit the floor on the run. He wouldn't be called unless it were an emergency and an emergency sixteen lightyears from Sol he did not need! He came into the comshack on the run and snapped, "Report!"

"Sir!" Sgt. (Sergeant was the least rank on a starship) Kim said. "We are at central service point. We find there was a ship here! It is not Sol design, nor is it Goombridgian!"

"Is it still in the area?" Todd asked.

"It is!" Kim replied.

"Have you tried contact?" Todd asked.

"No sir! Awaiting orders, Sir!" Kim said.

"Stop calling me sir, damn it!" Todd demanded. "Kim, try to raise them on radio and light beam. Everything we have. Send anything. Pi."

"Pie?" Kim asked.

"Three bleeps, a blat one bleep, pause, four bleeps, pause one bleep, pause, six bleeps. Four decimals should be enough," Todd said.

"Aye, Todd," Kim replied and punched some board controls. "Frequency?"

"Wide range static on the radio. Infra-red to ultra-violet on light," Todd replied.

They waited a moment longer and a voice came through the monitor in some strange, clicking language.

"They're drawing inward on the radio beam to a short wave. The equipment will follow it," Kim explained. He picked up the hand microphone.

"English, Espanol, Francaise, Duestch, Chinese, Portugesa," he said.

"Mas facil, which is easier," the voice came back.

Kim brought the visual scope up to where Todd could see the ship on the screen. It was disc shaped.

"How big is it?" he asked of Kim.

"It's at, let's see, projected ... ten kilometers. Perspective – about a hundred feet across," Kim said.

"A hundred four feet nine inches," a pleasant but slightly sibilant voice replied. "You are from Terra, yet we detect no weapons. That is good.

"I am called Truncd and am a member of the Feach race from the Maitan Galactic Empire. I am sorry Terra is a restricted world and that we may no closer approach nor may we make direct contact with you as we may with most cultures who have entered interstellar space."

"But why not?" Todd asked.

"Because you are unable to resolve problems among your own race," Truncd replied. "There are presently more than three thousand races in the empire and we all get along well. You can see what kind of problems you would bring."

"But we have a world government now!" Kim cried.

"Yes, but only because you wish to fight the Goombridgians, as you call them. Only you, the Goombridgians and the Taus reside in your present sphere. The Taus are not a contentious nor a violent race. You and the Goombridgians are."

"You seem to know a lot about us!" Todd said angrily. "Your refusing of contacts doesn't include spying?"

"Look into yourselves," Truncd replied. "You become suspicious because I know of you and do not accept you. You would be more suspicious if I *did* accept you.

"You are wrong to think others are like you. Surely you have learned by now that there is nothing one race has that others could logically want. All things are everywhere.

"I know of you because a man was abducted from your planet more than a hundred years ago by a race who had a small empire and who were much like you in some ways, but very different in most others. That Terran is a friend of the emperor.

"I am reptilian. My present crew consists of mammalian, reptilian, amphibian and even unclassifiable races. The fact I am reptilian would preclude trust from you. You shun any extended contact with the Taus because they are very different and you wish to war with the Goombridgians because they are so much like you in psychology as well as physically.

"I will tell you the Taus will be offered membership in the empire soon, but Terrans and Goombridgians may possibly never be allowed among us."

Kim was so angered he was about to explode, but Todd put a hand on his shoulder.

"I wish I could argue the point," Todd said. "I know much of what you say is true, but it is true of only a few of us. Most of us are not like that."

"I have met the Terran friend of the emperor and must agree that he would say the same," Truncd replied. "It is also quite true, I have no doubt. You seem a reasonable being and he most definitely is – well, usually. He has a wonderful sense of humor.

"Which ones are in charge?"

Todd thought a moment and said, "I see your point.

"We are changing. Maybe much too slowly, but we ARE changing! I'm working to make vast changes in one area myself and will do all I can to cause the disbanding of the military. It's the number one priority in my life.

"I've met a few Goombridgians and I can say that most of them don't want trouble."

"Only the ones in charge of their society want trouble, as you say, but they are the ones who chose those in authority," Truncd replied. "As it is true that you have chosen those in charge of your society. Both of your races seem unduly attracted to those who glorify war and violence.

"We could slap you down with almost no effort and throw them out, but how long would it be before you had the same types again in charge? What must change before you are allowed contact with others is something basic within yourselves and I don't know if you can do that. You have the basic desire for conquest, personal wealth, power, but have not the logic of mind to see that such things have no real value. You are a very compassionate people while at the same time you have an amazing capacity for cruelty.

"We have one such well-known race in the empire now. We are coming very close to being forced to quarantine them on their home planet, I think. They are racially dishonest. They have the greed for power and wealth."

Kim was glaring at the set, but Todd knew Truncd was merely speaking absolute truth. His goal in life was to avenge Old Mike Cogsworth, who was one of the few who actively fought those in power.

This was one of the things one couldn't find in any of the books! The contact they all knew must come had come to him and he was powerless – to think in those terms proved Truncd's point yet again – to do anything other than to tuck his tail between his legs and to try to look innocent.

Or to stand up to the facts!

"I see." He took a deep breath and asked, "Are *we* to be quarantined, then?"

"Only at such time as you begin to do damage to other beings and other places," Truncd replied. "We have seen that you avoid developing worlds, which is why you are not interfered with.

"Make no mistake that we will stop you if you ever change that policy! The race I earlier mentioned who is now causing so much trouble is one who was contacted much too early in their social development. Their social evolution stopped at the point of contact. It is now argued among scholars that they will never change as a result. It is also said they would have destroyed themselves many centuries ago had they not been contacted. They had the capacity to use nuclear devices against their own kind.

"The rule that no one interferes with a developing culture is number one in the empire. Number two is that there be no nuclear explosive devices or other polluting nuclear weapons, as they are too longterm in their effects. Your race still manufactures them when you know that beam weapons are much more efficient for the killing of each other and that energy weapons do not leave a price for countless future generations to pay in residual poisons and radiation."

Any arguments Todd had died at that point. He could see the shock and shame on Kim's face. Earth's military *did* insist on the stockpiling of explosive nuclear devices, as did Goombridge's, while both cultures knew full well that those devices were obsolete. It was only too true that a beam weapon was more efficient, as Truncd had said, "at killing each other" and they do not leave dangerous fallout around to kill people hundreds of years in the future.

What a hell of a mess!

"You say that an Earthman was a friend of the emperor a hundred years ago?" Todd asked. "I guess that's the reason we weren't quarantined when we first found the TTH drive?"

"He is still a friend of the emperor and even travels around with him when they explore new worlds," Truncd answered.

"Wait a minute! The emperor of thousands of worlds explores?!" Kim shouted. "Where does he find the time?"

"The emperor is merely a figurehead," Truncd answered. "He sort of sets things up to run themselves. The Maitan Galactic Empire is, as the Terran says, a giant trading guild that is run by machines. Even an emperor grows bored after a few hundred years."

"But, but you have immortality!?!" Kim asked, incredulously.

"I guess so, for all practical purposes," Truncd replied. "The

Terran and their friend, a Mentan and the emperor are the only ones who use it. The emperor because he must and the Terran and the Mentan because they are such close friends and companions. They have accepted the curse so Emperor Maita would have someone to go through this with."

"You say we're crazy?" Kim shouted. "And you would turn down *immortality*? You call it a *curse*?!"

Truncd laughed a hissing laugh. "Think about it," he said. "We use enough of it to keep us in good health, but I have no desire to live on and on. I would beg for death after awhile!"

Todd was grinning. "I think you're intelligent to refuse it," he said. "I would take it if I could limit it and die when I've done the things I've sworn to do, but I would refuse it as a forever thing."

"I think we could be friends," Truncd said. "It is too bad we may not. I wish you well, but I must go now. I am expected at Hospital shortly."

"You are ill?" Todd asked.

Truncd laughed again and replied, "No, I am a doctor. This is a hospital ship. We are returning to our home base from a planet that a plague was decimating. The Feach are known as the finest doctors and pharmacists in the galaxy.

"You see, we substitute our pride in that for the desire of conquest. We can each say we have had a direct hand in saving an entire race – and this is not the first. The Feach serve a definite purpose in existence.

"I wish you well."

"Wait!" Kim cried. "I know your name is Truncd. Mine is Kim and my commander here is Todd.

"When you say 'Mentan,' I think of a brain in a jar for some reason. I want to know what the Mentan looks like! Is it a mammal?"

"No," Truncd answered with the hissing laugh. "It is not a classifiable being. It is relatively small and has four tentacles and eyes on stalks. It resembles the Taus to an extent."

"And what are you like?" Todd asked. "You say 'reptile' and I can't picture it."

Truncd laughed again and Todd knew he would like the being no matter what he looked like.

"The Terran describes the Feach as looking like a `nine foot Tyrannosaurus rex,' which may mean something to you," Truncd said. "I must go."

There was a flash and the ship was gone.

Todd thought for a moment, then asked Kim who else knew about this.

"I called you on direct alert. Everyone else is sleeping until the new survey starts in three hours," Kim said. "The only ones awake are midship and won't know anything about it.

"Why?"

Todd ran the sensor and data recordings back to when Kim first spotted the alien ship, paused and sadly punched "erase" as Kim stared mouth-agape and wide-eyed.

"Kim, I know when you think of it you'll see we have no choice here. We must never tell anyone of this," Todd said very quietly. "If we were to say what we heard you can see what would happen."

"But ... I ... but...! But!!!" Kim cried. "But we'll be quarantined unless we change! Earth has to know!"

"Kim! Think!" Todd cried. "What will the military do if they hear any of this?"

"Why, they'll ... they would.... They'll say we have to spend every single dollar we can get our hands on for arms to defend ourselves and the fact we couldn't possibly defend against such an empire would make no difference," Kim said.

"Even worse," Todd said. "They'll say the reason the empire told us to get rid of the atomics is because they're afraid of them. They'll start to build thousands – millions – of the bombs and nuclear missiles, meaning we *will* end up quarantined!"

Kim groaned. "Todd, we can't, I mean I.... Space is my life!

They won't let us...."

"No. They won't bother us so long as we stay *away* from nuclear weapons and so long as we don't interfere with other cultures," Todd said. "It's really up to us how we come out of this.

"We have to work for reason. We can't do it if the whole lousy world is mad or scared or something.

"I hate to admit it, but what I'm picturing right now is me sitting across a table from a nine foot dinosaur telling jokes! I liked that guy!"

"I did too at the end, but the truth sort of hurts just the same. I could have strangled him for a while there," Kim said. "I wonder how hard it would be to strangle a dinosaur?"

"He'd pluck you off and step on you," Todd said. "Not one word about this. Agreed?"

"Yeah, Todd, you're right," Kim said. "Damn! The biggest thing that could ever happen to us and we have to keep mum about it!"

"That's the hard part," Todd agreed as he left the room. "I'm going to go back to bed to try to convince myself it was only a dream.

"Wake me for the scouting."

He went to his cabin and to bed again. It shows how able he was to control himself that he actually got some sleep.

Todd became a bit too philosophical for his own taste for the next few days. He was forced to accept what he was and what the race was and was becoming. If things continued as they were going it wasn't a rosy future.

Could man ever grow beyond this greedy, dirty, selfish, uncaring, cruel savage with technology into something finer? Was the human race what it was to be in the far future? Would they ever learn anything at all?

He could not, *must not*, believe that! That was to end it all because humanity as it now was *didn't* really deserve to continue.

Facts are facts! And some of those facts were people like Cogsworth, who could give a set of values to a young probably obnoxious kid prodigy. That set of values proved beyond the possibility of doubt that man could be much better. It was true the good was outnumbered a thousand to one by the mediocre and the good was probably also outnumbered ten to one by the bad, but that wasn't important. The good was there – and that was the all-important factor!

Todd, being Todd, then accepted that the long struggle, while almost impossibly difficult, was winnable. It wouldn't come in his lifetime, but that wasn't important, either. He could dream that some of it would come *because* of his lifetime! Hopefully he would have a family and his grandchildren could profit from his life.

No man could ask more. This wasn't a thing that came in such short time nor thought. It took the better part of four days of very intense introspection and a lot of honest intimidating self-examination. For the first time he realized something: It was very hard to tell oneself the truth about oneself because the mind refuses to see what doesn't fit its pattern. He had been far more truthful to others than to himself.

He now knew what he felt to be absolute truth to others was, in fact, blackly and flatly false. He was telling the truth as he saw it, but he didn't see it as it actually was. His lies were in the attempt to be truthful!

It confused him, but once he had sorted it all out he could prepare himself to defend against himself in the future. It was finally resolved, then he went about his work. Kim had several long conversations with him. They agreed to swear a statement, put it with the secondary tape of the whole "meeting" and to seal it in hopes it could some day be known. Kim was Korean in ancestry so had a great deal more natural patience than Anglo-Saxon Todd, but Todd would just have to bear with it. There was a hollow ache in him he knew would never go away so long as he lived – would in fact grow stronger. It was a loneliness born of knowing there were others "out there" whose company would be denied to him through no fault of his own.

Man longs to belong. There is a galactic society out there and it's only human to want to be a part of it. The loss Todd felt was as bad as that he felt upon hearing of Old Mike's death. The "Final Exam" was escape to him. He could get in that ship and could lose himself in the survey and the intricacies of flight.

He explored a system that had a lot of minerals but no life. He then went to another close system where he was called by Natalie Kormovich. There was a planet that was beginning to develop life, but nothing very far up the scale yet.

"We can land and meet in sterile suits," he told her. "We can then decide what we have here."

They made landfall on a wide rocky/sandy plain where Todd took out the large microscope.

"What will that show you?" Natalie asked.

"It will show the design-forms life will take, to an extent," Todd said. "The direction of the protein revolutions will show us whether this will be a dextro or a levo world. Mmmm. Sugar stain, please."

He stained the sugars in a piece of algae with the special dye, then looked at the telltale streaks.

"Levo," he said.

"How often is one found to be levo?" she asked.

"It seems to be chance. About fifty-fifty," he replied. "The importance is that we can't eat dextro in a lot of things, but the most ordinary thing can be used as a medicine or such.

"Sometimes.

"Let's get some pond scum to see what the animals will look like."

"You can tell?" she asked.

"In theory," Todd answered. "See the smaller things

developing in multicellular groupings? Ninety percent of them have tentacles. This planet has no large moons so the intelligence we find here in about two hundred million years will be like the Taus, more than likely. In theory. If you learn what to look for you can do all this stuff on a planet and not bother with taking samples."

"You lost me," Natalie protested. "What did you mean about the moon?"

Todd grinned through the plastic faceplate at her. "A large body close in space will cause tides that affect life variety," he explained. "Tides stir things and you know what agitation does to chemicals. You get variety.

"There are only the small tides caused by the sun here so there will be very little variety in form. There may be a lot of things with tentacles and all quite different, but there won't be many with claws or feet or such. That's the way it seems to go. This will be really different in a few million years!

"Your decision?"

"Planet classification "X", unique evolutionary precedent," she said. "Right?"

Todd smiled at her and said, "That's precisely what I'd do. Excellent job, Scout Kormovich!"

"We should leave surface immediately," she suggested. "I will appreciate it if you will come with me to the other two planets to show me some other ways to survey."

"Unless you find something really important it's best to find nothing at all," Todd said.

"Explain," Natalie said.

"If they have any reason to come to the system some ass will make it a point to come here "X" or not and will contaminate the world," Todd said, shaking his head. "Unfortunately, that's human nature."

"Should we bother to survey?" she asked.

"Oh, yes, cursorily," Todd replied. "There's always a slight chance that something will be there that we shouldn't overlook. A cursory will find anything spectacular."

"But I've never seen a system that wasn't spectacular and unique in one way or another!" Natalie said. "I hope I never do."

"You will, but they're unique in that it's so rare not to find any surprises or spectacular scenery."

"Nothing I have ever seen was more beautiful than twelve G two four," she said. "It's an ice world with very wide rings and ice moons. It's like fantastic jewels in black velvet when viewed from the direction of the sun."

Todd didn't approve of that type of shorthand, but held his tongue. After all, it wasn't a report. They checked out the two rocky, hot worlds, then returned to the mother. Todd took her to the lab section where he taught her how to use the scanning machinery recordings to spectrograph the planets. He took out several older finds to show her what various ores looked like in various light wavelengths.

"I would like to discuss some things with you when you have the free time," Todd said. "I see in you the makings of one of the finest scouts in the service. A few years ago Old Mike took charge of me and taught me one hell of a lot more than any books or anything else ever could. I want to pass some of that on to you and I want to explain some philosophy."

She smiled at him and he felt a strange warm glow, but caught himself. He was a normal man and all that, but he had sworn an oath to himself so would not allow himself to become involved with anyone until he had done what he set out to do.

They decided they had the time so they moved around to the next survey center loci where they mapped four more systems. The set method was to move a certain distance from Earth, follow a circle of equal distance from Sol, then move outward another couple of light years. They made a three quarter circle, leaving a cone in the direction of Goombridge out, as Goombridge did with Earth. Todd wished they were sharing the explorations. It would make it better for all concerned, but that wasn't human – or, if the news could be believed, Goombridgian – nature.

Maybe Truncd was right. Maybe they'd never change.

They then sat around in the laboratory section conference room to discuss what they'd found. "We have to tighten all this up for the files, then you get a little vacation," Todd said. "The First Attempt" goes into overhaul and refit when we get back to Luna Base. Sixty days.

"I'll expect each of you to stay cold sober and to not spend your time with the opposite sex while on leave!"

They all laughed and Ella asked, "Are you suggesting that we spend the time with the same sex? Hmmm?"

Todd was ready.

"Well, no one would come back pregnant!" he pointed out.

"I didn't know you worried about becoming pregnant, Sir," she shot back, smirking. "But after looking over your psychological records I can understand why you would be confused.

"You see, it takes a male and a female. Two males, no matter how they try – and there are lots of ways to try – can't do it!"

"They can do it, but it definitely won't result in pregnancy!" Todd shot back.

"You apparently know more about that than I do, Sir!" she said grinning broadly.

He should have learned by now not to challenge her like that! He had no answer.

The group joked and laughed awhile, then they each went to his or her own recorder to give their own analysis of what had been discovered and what it meant, then played the recorders into the main computers. The computers cross-filed all reports, made a "composite sketch" of the system and of each world, then made an overall printout of the trip to present to

Luna Base Command with a color-code, red for "X", blue for usable, green for special attention and so forth. Kim came to his cabin with a long sheet that had a large amber streak across it.

"We seem to have a bit of a problem," he said. "It seems the computer wants to inform anyone using it that there's a space of twenty four point three seven minutes for which it has no data. It has checked with outship sensory and finds the same problem.

"What do I do? If anyone checks this will leave one hell of a lot to be explained! If we're going in for overhaul at the end of this trip we have a real problem with a capital "P"!"

Todd grinned. He was glad he had learned how to use – and to misuse – the machines.

"C'mon," he said. "I'll show you a trick Mike Cogswell showed me."

They went to the main console where Todd called up the time in question. The machine flashed "No Data! Error!"

He punched "Edit: Insert Data" and waited.

"You can't insert past time on these machines," Kim said.

Todd grinned at him and waited while the machine clicked and flickered a moment, then printed "Program Incomplete. No Data Revision: Error! Warning! Error!"

Todd printed "Recall program amber: Program Error #35: Insert Corrected Program."

There was an extended pause, then the machine printed "Program Error #35: Retest InSystem/ OutSystem Sensory Input. Autodata transfer requested. Orders Please."

Todd printed "Retest InSystem/OutSystem Sensory Input. File Corrected Report as Insert ~ Recall: Program Amber ~ Report All Damage and/or material deterioration as Current Time. Exception: Damage at Recall Program Amber Real Time Displaced To Current Time Only."

The computers printed "Compliance Time Differential. Sensory Input Test Two Minutes. Recall SPD#35INSRT

Program 24.37 Minutes. Orders Please."

Todd printed "Use Time Sequence Doppler Test Visual Sensors and report on: >Recall Program Amber< only. Complete time sequence as used. Overwrite. Return To Other Duties Current Standard Time."

The machine printed "Complying. Please Input All Data Driver Two (2) Until Screen Clock Is At Zero (0). Thank You."

"How did you do that!?" Kim asked.

"Anytime you have to erase something and want to account for the time give vague orders about a test," Todd instructed. "The important thing is to know which tests the machine is programmed to make that are to be made in override sequence. The machine has standing orders to make the tests only when the boards are clear.

"Number thirty five is external sensors, which are modemed in so are sometimes lost when the computer is doing something else. The data disk will have unused space for the time, but there will be nothing there except the message to the machine to input from the memory of the sensor computers when it's free.

"Such messages are sometimes lost, so number thirty five can be recalled in any form. The computer only knows, one, that it is to input sensory computer data in that space, two, that it has no specified message as to when to take the data and, three, that the operator can specify a time when there's a glitch to have it put in that space. There was no information on the sensory computer disk for the time requested, ergo, there's a damaged disk, ergo, a glitch.

"Now we have to go to the Sensory Section computers, which we can directly insert, and have the information now being taken placed on the space on the disk there through modem. The machines don't know what we're doing so will simply do it, leaving no gap nor any memory of a gap. After all, glitches *do* happen! That's why there's a repair process sequenced into the thing!"

Kim grinned and said, "Let me hope I never get myself into a courts martial offense when you aren't around! I thought we'd both end up against the wall!"

"I fully intend to eventually see someone stood against the wall, but *you* ain't it!" Todd murmured as they went to Sensory Section to finish their subterfuge.

He couldn't know how very close that time was to be!

Chapter five

"I don't mean to sound unreasonable," Todd said, "but there are some things I can't accept on your say-so. I think you have one hell of a lot of nerve to try to hand me that!

"I don't like to pull rank either, but I can and will do that when necessary, too! I'm a full commander and you're a lousy sergeant and a bureaucrat. Hold that thought firmly in mind. I can have your ass busted to latrine orderly so fast it'll spin your tiny little brain out the top of your bald head! No one reaches your age as a sergeant unless they're immensely stupid, so please try to concentrate. I will now ask as though for the first time.

"Where are the safety and overhaul records for the ship of which I am the officer in charge – "The First Attempt" – record's number ATP four thirty one A?"

The sergeant at the desk simply repeated, "I do not have those records at this time."

"Then push the keys on your little computer and have a printout for me within two minutes. You're the officer in charge of those records and are required to give them to the CO of any ship who requests them.

"Get them for me now, Private!"

"I have higher orders not to!" the sergeant claimed. "And you can't bust me! I'm following orders from higher than you!"

"Then you can tell me whose orders you're following," Todd snapped.

"I have orders not to reveal that information," the sergeant replied.

"Then you realize that I am forced to assume you have no such orders," Todd said. "Guards! MP's! On the double!"

"What are you doing!?" the sergeant cried as two of the guards came into the office, saluted Todd, then looked a question at him.

"Place this man under arrest on insubordination charges," Todd demanded. "Watch him carefully. I may be lodging treason charges later if what I suspect materializes. I'll officially endorse the papers before I leave the building. Take him out and place him in confinement."

The guards moved to either side of the sergeant, saluted and started to take him out.

"One more little thing," Todd said. "He is now demoted from holding any rank whatever, so will be removed from the service without honor at the very least.

"I didn't make full commander by tolerating petty bureaucrats, Hotshot! You types always go a little bit too far and end up with me being forced to remove you from obstructing me. You'll find that you're required by order three one one two four point two one to tender full information to any officer who's refused a reasonable request as to by whom and for what reason that request is refused.

"You would definitely be required to know of that rule to hold your job, so you were merely obstructing me when you refused the information as to who gave you your orders.

"Any other officer here would have merely gone over your head for the information. You're a victim of your own petty little rules. I go by the book and I'm good at it. I wrote most of the book, so I know exactly what it says.

"I hope you're near your retirement. You lose it all!

"Don't you feel powerful? Isn't it fun showing up all the big brass who got the promotions you should have gotten yourself?

"All right, take this garbage out of my sight. Have another assigned to this information desk. I'll wait here until someone reports for the duty."

They again saluted him and spun the sergeant around to lead him out as he started a protest.

As soon as they were out of the room Todd sat at the desk

console where he expertly punched the code for his records. He had once been records officer on a ship, so knew the computers inside out. He knew how to override the added commands and soon had his printout. He was reading it when the new man came in.

"You aren't to use those machines!" the man cried.

"You weren't here to stop me, so it's no problem of yours," Todd said. "Before you say one more word to me, Sergeant, ponder on the fact that your predecessor at this desk is all alone in his cell and might appreciate company!"

The sergeant looked confused and scared, but merely saluted him.

"Don't worry about it, Sergeant," Todd said. "I know how to use the computers. There's no record anyone got this information, so you can say the twenty eight sheets of paper were gone when you arrived. The smartest thing you can do is forget you saw me with this data. You don't know what it is in any case and there is no question I have clearance for anything that might be here."

The sergeant grinned and said, "I wonder why that guy didn't stay here until I got in? Anybody could've come in here and used the machines. Good thing nobody without clearance knows those codes and anyone *with* the codes is automatically authorized!

"Don't he know there's classified stuff in these machines?

"Oh, well. Everything seems shipshape. Now where did I leave my book?"

He walked past Todd, picked a book off the top of a file case, then sat to read, ignoring Todd's presence altogether.

"Good man, that replacement officer," Todd said as he shoved the report papers inside his shirt and walked out. "Probably'll go a long way in the service. Knows when he's walked into a setup and has the sense to avoid the trap!"

He took the papers and returned to his ship to study them. Everything seemed normal to him. He couldn't understand why the fuss about giving him the records.

He flipped back through the stuff. His eye was drawn to a strange entry in the furniture area. He thought for a few minutes, then leaned back and said, "So that's it!"

"Todd?" the intercom wakened him from his doze in the chair.

"Yes?" he answered.

"Can I come in there and disturb you?" It was Admiral Pwester, Todd's friend from the Services Administration offices.

"Sure, Carl, come on up. I'm in the library."

He waited for about two minutes until Pwester came in to throw his hat on the table, pour himself a cup of hot coffee and sit across the table from Todd.

"I got an urgent from the old man," Carl said. "You have his aide in the brig, busted and're about to charge him with treason or some such crap. What's going on? I'm supposed to smooth it all over."

"Not this one, Carl," Todd answered. "I've had it with this intrigue stuff. It's gone too far when some prissy little half-assed bureaucrat sergeant can thumb his ugly pug nose at a commander, break all the rules, be obstructive and insubordinate and get away with it because the old man wants to play a silly game. That sergeant gets busted and mustered out on a DD or I bring treason charges against him. We go to full court to hear him say he was acting on the old man's orders. The old man can explain why he would restrict a commander from seeing the safety reports on his own ship. Even he doesn't have the power to do that!"

"Okay, he doesn't, but why take it out on a sergeant?"

"Because the sergeant is much older than I am and is due for retirement wherein the Terran taxpayers will have to reward him in continuity for being a jerk. He was enjoying the act and WAS, in reality, insubordinate.

"Because I won't permit someone who has been in the

service for thirty years – without any advance in the last twenty five – living off the funds that should be available to those who have, in fact, earned it.

"Because if he was competent at any job whatever in the time he's been in the services he would be much higher than a desk sergeant and because he's so popular with everyone who's been in contact with him that they all ran immediately to his defense.

"Carl, you know the type. He's the old man's aide and yes man because he's thoroughly hated by everyone else. He's the little yuck who runs to the old man to report any silly little technical infraction he can find and to enter it in a good man's records. He's a spiteful little failure who will do all in his power to cause trouble for those with ability.

"He's someone who should've been thrown out of the services after he proved unable to advance twenty five years ago! He's the result of letting politicians like the old man run these things.

"I don't understand why I'm justifying my position to you. The answer's a flat NO!"

Pwester stared at him for a full minute, then said, "Now that that's off your chest, what's really the matter?"

"What would you say if you were to suddenly discover someone had installed a luxury suite in a ship under your command, then tried to hide that fact from you?" Todd asked.

"Did they?" Pwester asked.

"And then some," Todd replied.

"Who's going to be your guest?" Carl asked.

"Probably some politician who doesn't have legal clearance to step one foot inside the ship, Carl. I'm in the position of having to thoroughly check every person who comes aboard to find the ringer. If they could've kept the fact I'm going to have a guest from me it would've been easy. Now I'll find out about it."

"So? Throw them out!" Pwester suggested.

"It's not that easy," Todd said. "Think about it. It takes the subversion of at least one of my crew and collusion with the old man to, in effect, commit open treason.

"Carl, I'm going to have to bring the old man up on charges. This is unforgivable. We know what we have with him and we have no idea what will be next, but I'm one of the people who rewrote those thousands of rules. It's well-known I'm a stickler. The old man is doing this as a personal challenge to me. If he thinks he can get around the laws we've installed he's going to find he chose the wrong rule and the wrong person to challenge in any way.

"This kind of thing is capital, you know. I won't hesitate to put the old man in front of a firing squad. I mean it! If you've got any influence at all with him you'd do him a big favor see that he withdraws the furniture and forgets about it!"

"I don't have any influence with him at all," Carl said. "He hates my guts because I'm as loyal to the fleet as you are and have voted to overrule some things you really wouldn't believe from that ass.

"I'll simply report you are going to follow the book, page and paragraph, and that interference will result in a treason charge against anyone who sticks their nose into it. If he doesn't have the sense to drop it you'll be seeing him in court and will have him by the short hairs. All we'll lose is a known quantity. It's not impossible that we could get a good man in his stead."

"As long as it's up to the politicians we're going to have the same thing," Todd said dryly.

"You're probably right," Carl answered. "I wish you luck. I'm behind you all the way."

They made some small talk for a few minutes, then Pwester left to go back to his command. Todd sat to think out what he had to do now. The ship was released as of the following morning, which was why he wanted the reports. He would have to work out some way to locate the imposter and also the crew member – or crew members – who were in on the conspiracy.

Todd went to the ship as soon as it was released to move it onto the pad himself. He would put out a call that no one was to come aboard until the following day when he would assign each of the eighty four in the permanent crew an individual time of entry and assignment. That would make it possible for him to greet each one personally. He could use the meetings to detect a number of things. This might prove to be very interesting.

He used the inboard sensors on the empty ship to determine that no one had been smuggled in before it left repair bay, then went to the suite that had been fixed up for his "guest's" use. The sensors in the room had been disconnected, so he reconnected them himself before rechecking the ship.

He sealed the entire ship except for the single entrance port that was generally used only by himself or visiting brass. He contacted each member of the regular crew by computer link to give instructions as to how they were to come aboard. One every five minutes – through his single port. He would be at a desk there where he would identify and check in each person who came aboard. If anyone was too anxious to help him he would have his culprit.

He sat up a couple of other little traps, too. It was good to have come up through the ranks and to have a few skills of his own.

He had checked in nine of his crew when a small light came on at the edge of his desk. It was a light with the number four on it, so he turned on the remote sensor security view of emergency hatch four on the far side of the ship. Evans, security detail, was trying to open the hatch. It was magnetically sealed, there was no way anyone could open it except by override and Todd had the console keyed only to himself.

He showed no haste in checking Plotkins, Vera, biologist 1st class, scientific survey team in. He then leisurely closed the port from the outside ramp and strolled casually and unhurriedly around the ship. A ground car was there and two men were waiting by the hatch.

He went back around to climb aboard, bringing Sgt. Grovich, a known and trusted officer, aboard with him. He handed Grovich a hand laser as he told him to come along. He then punched the code that would allow the hatch to be opened and closed the entrance hatch again. He and Grovich arrived as Evans was helping the two through the hatch.

"Evans!" Todd shouted.

Evans spun, grabbing for his sidearm. Todd shot him where he stood, then trained the weapon on the two at the hatch.

"Take one deep breath and you die where you stand!" Grovich shouted at them. "You're under arrest on a charge of espionage against the Terran Space Fleet. Anything you say or do will be recorded by the ship sensors and will be used in evidence against you in a military court."

"Do you know who I am?!" one of the prisoners snapped.

"I quite frankly don't give a diddly-damn," Todd snapped back. "This is a fully classified ship that you attempted entering surreptitiously through an emergency hatch with the aid of a crew member who was subsequently shot down as he tried to assassinate his commander. You and all who were in this conspiracy to commit treason against the Terran Space Fleet will be tried and, upon conviction, stood against a wall and shot. I suggest very pointedly that you do not again open your damned mouth until you have benefit of counsel.

"Captain Grovich, take these two to the brig and put a full time guard on them. Instructions are to shoot at any sign of resistance by these traitors."

"Aye, sir!" Captain (who was a sergeant until one minute ago) Grovich snapped. "Come on, you scum. Give me an excuse to fry your asses! Just make one small move I don't tell you to!"

Grovich led the two away while Todd went back to pass the rest of the crew aboard after assigning two of those already there to remove Evan's body to the med room.

When all were aboard he called the base security box to say he was holding two prisoners aboard he would transport to Luna base for trial.

"Sir!" the answer came. "If you will turn them over to us we will handle the affair."

"To tell you the truth," Todd snarled, "they could never have entered this base without your collusion. They're gonna be taken to Luna and anyone – *anyone* – who had any part of this will be charged and tried for treason. They will then be put against the wall and shot!

"You may wish to consider going AWOL. No one is immune from these charges. Not even the old man.

"We leave in ten minutes and you had better not try to stop us. We have much better weapons than you. I assure you I won't hesitate to use them."

Luna base had been completed only eight years ago and was one of the finest facilities the Terran Fleet had. It had an entrance port that would easily allow even so large a Mother Class ship as "The First Attempt" to be totally enclosed in the plastic dome. The landing dome was a semi-sphere with one half on a track that would allow it to open upward from the runway with motors. As soon as the ship was drawn inside the dome shut. The dome itself didn't carry an air supply, but had connector tunnels that did. The ship was hooked to the tunnels where one moved about freely – taking into consideration the lessened gravity.

On the ship itself one wore a magnetic uniform that was held to the "floor" by a form of broadcast magnetism that made one comfortable but, as the ubiquitous signs said, "He who pours liquids cleans up the mess."

Todd went out and down the ramp first where he checked

the credentials of the four MP's who were waiting to take his two prisoners off the ship. A tribunal was to be called and a trial held to determine if the interlopers should be tried for capital espionage. Todd would act as prosecutor. That was another side-job he'd held coming up through the ranks.

The two were led into the room for trial about two hours later where the three judges gasped in unison. One of them called Todd over to the judges' table and wrapped her hand over the computer voice-activated input.

"Commander Todd! Do you understand who these two men are?" she asked.

"They are two unauthorized persons who were being allowed into a classified ship by an officer who subsequently attempted to assassinate his CO. Me," Todd replied shortly.

"They are senators Hoshito and Rivera!" she said.

"I fail to see any connection with that and with the fact they were acting as espionage agents," Todd replied. "If you think for one picosecond the fact they're politicians excuses treasonous conduct you're very sadly mistaken, Major Polk."

"The panel respectfully requests that you drop charges against these two defendants," Major Self-Houser said.

"The charges are correct as filed and will be pursued to their completion," Todd returned. "It is not in the best interest of the services that espionage is given acceptance for any reason."

"My esteemed colleagues and I have received a request from Commanding Officer of Space Fleet Services that all pending charges against these two defendant be dropped," Commander Fletcher said. "Barring legal claims to prove danger or damage to the service we have voted to comply with that request in unanimous vote. This court orders that the defendant be returned to Earth and released."

Todd had done his homework well.

"I, Commander Robert Cole Todd, do hereby declare the actions of this tribunal treasonous under order number three eleven point two of the revised service code. No testimony has yet been heard and decisions of that order are expressly denied by said codes.

"Rule three eleven point two section seven B reads, for the tribunal's enlightenment: `Any act of a court or tribunal which would tend to place said court or tribunal in a position that would suggest accessorization with treasonous acts shall result in the charge of treason to that court or tribunal.'

"Rule three eleven point five section one A reads: `Release and/or lessening of prosecution of any person or persons charged with deliberate treasonous acts WITHOUT DULY CERTIFIED TESTIMONY TAKEN OF ANY AND ALL WITNESSES AGAINST SAID ACTS shall be considered treasonous and shall be prosecuted under rule three eleven point two.'

"The full section is fourteen pages in length, but this is the section to which I refer. Treason is a capital offense. I beg that your honors carefully reconsider your last remarks in light of this rule.

"The rule also contains a strong provision as to how higher authority intervention may and may not be used. As you have also mentioned actions by the Commanding Officer of the Space Fleet Service, I demand, as property of the courts under rule fifty two thirty one point six that those requests be turned over to me for possible prosecution of the originator on the charge of high treason.

"Again, I strongly urge this tribunal carefully to reconsider and withdraw the ruling which is in direct contravention of law as advised."

The judges put their heads together, talked animatedly for a moment, then took the "Laws and Regulations" book out to study. They then declared a recess for one hour. When they again met it was foregone that the two would be held in full trial for espionage. Depositions were taken and sworn. Todd, Grovich and the tapes of the security cameras were entered.

It was quickly established quite definitely that the two senators would be tried and convicted of espionage, but not for treason.

The tribunal tried to gloss over the old man's involvement, but that didn't work, either.

Todd went with Grovich back to the ship where he made further arrangements to run the status survey of the planet discovered somewhat nearer to the center of the spiral arm. He could easily time it to be back in time for the trials. On Earth. With Todd as prosecutor.

Well, he was ready! No one could say Robert Cole Todd was ever unprepared for whatever he got himself into!

This wasn't the time to start gloating. The hardest part was ahead and mistakes wouldn't be overlooked. The politicians would jump on any chance to stop these proceedings "Like a duck on a Juney bug," as Todd's mother had often said.

Time was on his side. He would have time to prepare, time to think, time to even rehearse. If people could be made to understand this was a conspiracy by Commander (Hon.) Karel Thames Grimes to turn the services into a purely military operation under the auspices of those crooked politicians they would rise against him and a new order would take its place in man's history.

"If you believe that, I have some real estate on Venus that I'll sell cheap!" Todd mumbled.

Well, a survey trip would give them exactly as much time as it would allow him. Government Center would have thousands of petty little lawyers they could assign to finding the least flaw, the least thing he had overlooked.

"I'm going to ruin them all! I swear that to you, Old Mike!" Todd said and didn't care that people turned to stare at him.

They had rewritten the rule book. He had been patient enough to wait so long they couldn't revise the laws without a big public stink.

He hoped.

He arrived at his hotel to find some good news and some bad. Good, because it was deserved and bad, because it hit him hard where he least expected it.

Natalie Kormovich was now S Commander Kormovich and had a ship. Pwester was moving into head of administration, first man under Grimes (Who must be fuming!) and Natalie was his "most qualified subject" choice for command of the "Ecstasy".

Carl jumped her several grades and was going on instinct just as Cogsworth had done with him. He certainly couldn't argue with the choice, but the feeling of loss placed him where he wanted to. Was he to lose everything he had learned to care about? Was this another slap that life would give him?

People always looked at him and said he had the universe by the tail. He had everything anyone could ever want in life!

So why did life always dangle it out to him, then jerk it away if he reached for it?

Chapter six

The trip from Luna Base was strange. Todd hadn't really ever dated Natalie or even spent very much time with her, but he was somehow aware she wasn't aboard. The newest scout pilot was an experienced pilot who had come up through the ranks all the way. He would be good, competent – all the things a commander could possibly want. He was brilliant as an inventor of little things to make the job safer and easier.

Todd felt himself resenting the fellow and knew that wasn't logical. It wasn't this man's fault Natalie had been promoted!

He outgrew his resentment on the first scout trip. He was following the sensors in on a planet that wasn't following any of the rules. It looked like a normal type three, which would make it much like Earth and even had a small moon. A very small moon.

The trouble was, according to his sensors, the orbit was very eccentric. The planet seemed to have a heavy spot or something that made it wobble like one of those trick basketballs with the weight on one side. The moon seemed to have perched dead over the wobble point, or center of gravity, so Todd was extremely careful about landing.

The next thing was that there seemed to be extreme tides and that shouldn't happen with that moon geostationary. There should *not* be that much of a tide!

Todd read into the recorder that the planet must be of very light elements with the only large deposit of anything heavy at the wobble spot. The moon, on the other hand, must be quite heavy in relation to the planet.

The spot he landed on was normal enough rock that even had some lead in it and he wasn't near the wobble point! He couldn't figure what would possibly be heavy enough to cause the anomaly.

He flew to the wobble point where he noticed that gravity

was, if anything, the slightest bit *less* there.

This was becoming scary, so he flew to the system where the new scout was surveying and called him.

"Tab?" he radioed. "I have a real puzzle when you're through here. It's anomalous enough to scare me, so let's buddy out the system, okay?"

Captain Tab McGrew (That was his name) said that if Todd would survey the fourth and last planet here they would go directly over.

They were soon enough back to the system and were standing off the planet in question when Todd heard McGrew whistle.

"That is one *weird* baby!" Tab radioed. "That thing seems to be revolving around a point at the surface!

"What's the theory, Doctor?"

"I thought the planet must be light elements and the moon heavy," Todd said. "Spectrographs show normal constituency for the planet, though. That's only surface and doesn't necessarily mean a whole heck of a lot.

"I landed and found the gravity at the wobble point is point oh oh four percent less than at ninety degrees and is in that big plain on the equator about two hundred miles from those flattened mountains to the west."

They spent a few minutes doing extensive sensor checks with the computers, but didn't find much.

"The point is now located in the ocean. It's moved four or five hundred miles in a couple of hours. Could the planet have a gaseous center with a spherical core that rolls around in it?" Todd asked.

"Not bloody likely!" Tab shot back. "As close to the surface as the center of gravity must be? It would break through ten billion years or so ago!"

"Notice the moon?" Todd pointed. "Perfectly round. Nothing is that perfect. Like a polished chrome ball bearing.

"Maybe it *is* chrome. That would make it heavy and would

make it damned valuable. Can't make TitChroPlat without chrome.

"I'm going after a sample!"

He started to hit the thrusters when he heard McGrew scream, "NO!" so withdrew his hand.

"Think of something?" Todd asked.

"I thought that no natural body could be that perfectly round or that perfectly polished," Tab said.

"An artifact? Here? A space station of some sort?" Todd asked incredulously. "It's almost a hundred miles thick, for crying out loud!"

"Not impossible," Tab said. "What else could make a perfect sphere in space? Is there anything natural that could do it?"

"Well, it could be a frozen ball of some liquid," Todd said. "Something that condensed around a small core, then froze."

"Without a bulge from the planet's gravity?" Tab asked.

"Yeah, it would definitely have a tidal bulge," Todd agreed. "The only other thing it could be is something liquid with such a strong gravity that it froze smooth. Gravity would make it smooth if it had enough. Mercury?"

"With that much gravity?" Tab asked. "You know what I think?"

"What's that? I'm sure as all get-out open for ideas!" Todd said dryly.

"I think we're looking at our first discovery of a neutron mass!" Tab said. "Nothing else, and I do mean nothing else, could approach that much gravity!"

"And I almost landed on it!" Todd said. "I'd be spread in an invisibly thin layer across the whole thing!"

"You'd reflect prettily!" McGrew said. "You got your name in the history books again, Kid! Way to go!"

"I could have had my name in the obituaries at the same time!" Todd cried. "You'd think I could have figured it! Wait!"

There was a silence for a few minutes.

"I told the computers we found a sphere that's very brightly reflective, perfectly round plus or minus nothing, nearly a hundred miles thick and has strong gravitational effects on a large planet, which it seems to be following in mutual orbital eccentricity with ... ahhhh!"

There was a chattering sound over the radio.

"It first has a big `Do not approach! Danger!' warning, and now wants to know the mean distance from the planet. Here. I'd say a hundred sixty thousand miles?"

"Yo!" Tab said. "Triangulates at one sixty six five."

There was another pause, then a chatter.

"Suggest mass of satellite double that of planet, thus large distortional bulge. Satellite mass/ volume indicates neutron mass. Approach closer than twelve thousand nine hundred miles in a Manta Scout Class will result in total destruction of ship," Todd reported. "Well, we have to record this one on all sensor. I'm glad there's nothing else in this system."

"Why?" Tab asked.

"Because you can bet this place will be put on itineraries for fifty kinds of scientists and they'd screw up any other planets in the system," Todd replied.

"I'd heard that about you. I'm glad to be aboard, Boss! I'm tired of the way those asses screw up everything they touch!" Tab said. "I'll have to check with you about how I can get away with sort of rearranging my survey reports."

"I can show you some neat little tricks," Todd replied. "I've got everything I can find a sensor or camera for."

"See you aboard Mama!" Tab said and was gone.

Todd "jumped" and was just behind Tab at "The First Attempt".

They spent quite a few hours in meetings, then took "The First Attempt" in as close as they dared to use the big ship's more powerful equipment on the moon. Everyone took their own personal pictures through the big scope.

"We'll stay in this system for awhile to see if we can make something that will withstand that gravity," Todd suggested.

They used the computers to try to design a landing craft, but discovered it wasn't possible with anything they could come up with. No known material would withstand that force. It would be compressed into nothing.

"We can get to within a couple of thousand miles with a ship that can handle the thrust to escape and that's that," McGrew said. "Care if I try something?"

"What?" Todd asked.

"I want to drop a big H-bomb on it," Tab said. "If we can blow a little piece off of it.... Just think! A piece of that thing one cubic inch would weigh about twenty thousand *tons* on Earth!"

Todd remembered what Truncd had said about nuclear devices and he got a look that said volumes from Kim.

Then he thought of something else.

"Sure, go ahead," he answered and watched Kim start to say something, then look a question at him.

He smirked.

They made the countdown, watching the craft with the big bomb drop with ever-increasing speed toward the moon. There was a sudden very small flash a short distance from the surface, then nothing.

"What happened?" Ella asked.

"The H-bomb is set off with a fission bomb," Todd said. "The plutonium in the fission bomb was compressed to critical mass at about the time the whole rocket collapsed in on itself. At the speed it was going it was so close to the moon that the vapors and such produced were drawn on to the moon.

"No bang. I expected that. Not even an H-bomb has enough power to escape that thing! I'll admit I didn't consider neutron mass when I was there and almost committed suicide by approaching that thing, but I've sort of computed things about it by comparing masses of the moon and that of the planet.

"On Earth, the gravity scales at thirty two feet per second squared at surface. That moon at surface calculates to over eighteen hundred fifty *miles* per second squared! If you fell off a one foot ladder there you'd hit the surface moving seven hundred miles per hour! That's like flying into a solid steel wall at seven hundred miles per hour. A rather gooey mess, wouldn't you say?"

"Geez!" Ella exclaimed. "Don't bring the result to my surgery! I couldn't even identify it!"

"We wouldn't have a crane that would pick it up against that gravity," Tab said. "I sort of thought there wouldn't be very much happening, but I hoped. We proved a lot of theories with the bomb and that's what I wanted to do."

"Take all our nuclears, put them in one rocket, and let's see if we can make any effect," Todd suggested.

"It'll be the same," Tab dismissed.

"We won't know that unless we try," Kim said and went out. He had seen that Todd wanted to dump all the nuclears and this was a perfectly safe way to do it.

Captain Tab McGrew cocked his head to the side, then grinned. When he was where no one else could hear he whispered, "Dump the military crap, then we forget to take on more on Luna Base?" he asked.

Todd grinned.

They watched the rocket move toward the moon, saw a flash that was the slightest bit brighter than the first, then nothing.

"Did we record it well?" Todd asked.

"Yes sir! All sensors on!" Kim said.

"Then we can go home," Todd said. "I say the experiment was a roaring – well, a mini-flashing success!"

"But all it did was to get rid of all the bombs!" Ella said.

"But we now know for a fact that we can't affect that thing with anything we have!" Todd said. "That little thing leaves us powerless. Sort of makes you think, doesn't it?

"Head for home!"

As they landed at the large port outside of Government City Todd couldn't help but be aware of the curiosity and even open hostility with which they were met. He punched the news of the past twelve days, the time since they left Luna Port for the planetary survey. The indicted senators had been in the headlines steadily. The news people had taken the side of the service that espionage was espionage. No one could figure the purpose of their actions, though there was speculation.

The full senate had attempted to pass a new set of laws that would let its members off, but the press had yelled ex post facto so long and loud they backed off. The old man tried to make an executive decision not to prosecute, which brought the press down on him full strength. He had a subpoena to appear at the trial of the two senators.

The intercom link buzzed and Pwester came up to the quarters.

"Well, Todd, you warned him," Carl said as he poured himself a cup of coffee. "The trial starts in the morning. I can tell you flatly that it's going to be a long, hard row to hoe. The old man is furious, but I think he's scared, too. He was almost nice to me today.

"Do you know what's happened since you left?"

"I've read the news," Todd answered. "I hoped it wouldn't go nearly this far."

"What isn't reported in the news is that a whole conspiracy has been unearthed and we're going to spring it on them at the trial," Carl said. "You have no idea how big this really is!

"I'm going to let you discover most of it as you go. Your original case gives you some great openings, so maybe you can shorten the ordeal. We've arranged to subpoena a total of nine senators, the old man, his aide and several other political big shots. Maybe Grimes will screw up enough for you to make short work of him.

"I think the other senators being there will give you a hint as to what's going on.

"The press is behind us while the people are being held in a balance as to where their loyalties will go. The taxpayers might like to know what their money's really going for – and no more hints.

"Tell me about the trip."

Todd knew it would be useless to question Pwester further, but he *was* interested!

The following morning he was in the court where they took a full day of filing and refusing motions. It was after noon the day after that the actual trial began.

"Senator Hoshito," Todd demanded. "Who was in this conspiracy with you and Senator Rivera?

"Let me explain to you here that there are more important issues here than minor espionage against two senators who should know better. I wouldn't be adverse to granting you and Senator Rivera immunity if you will cooperate with this court."

"I refuse to answer any questions under my rights as a Terran citizen," the senator responded.

"Very well," Todd replied. "The prosecution calls Captain Grovich."

"Objection!" the defense attorney cried.

"On what grounds?" the tribunal chief judge asked.

"Cross examination!" snapped the attorney.

"What? You can't *cross* examine a witness who doesn't testify!" the judge snapped shortly. "*Cross* examination is examination of statements presented in direct examination!

"Where did you go to school?"

That defense attorney looked puzzled and sat. He had quite a list of questions to ask the senator that would work very well as propaganda. His strategy to plead the fifth (He didn't have a clue as to where that old expression came from) had come back to smack him in his capped teeth!

Grovich came to the swearing-in stand to hand the judges a sworn affidavit. The judges passed it along, read it, then nodded. The bailiff placed the tape from the security cameras on "The First Attempt" into the playback machine.

"This is the security-sealed camera view of the things that transpired on the date in question," Todd said. "The court has confirmed and directed the removal and handling of this evidence. Captain Grovich will please explain the actions taking place as well as those that came about before and after the tapes.

"Captain Grovich, please present as briefly as possible. The recorded evidence should be self-explanatory for the largest part."

Grovich moved near the machine, picked up the handheld remote control unit, turned to the judges and stated, "I was in the process of reporting for duty on my assigned ship "The First Attempt", a survey ship of the Terran Space Service, on the date of July seven, two thousand one hundred and twenty nine A.D. when I was called by Commander Todd to enter the ship with him as a guard and special security officer. He gave me a defense sidearm laser model seven twelve and indicated to me there was a severe problem at emergency entrance escape port four. The security system had reported it had detected a break-in in progress, thus the use of myself, as I was on interview with the commander at that moment and time was critical in such a case.

"I informed Commander Todd that the system was automatically compensatory. I explained that it would not open from the outside unless keyed from the inside control, as Commander Todd was aware. The board had indicated the attempt to manually open the hatch, as the commander showed me, explaining that he had some foreknowledge of a type that would indicate the possibility of sabotage or worse to the ship and its personnel.

"Commander Todd ordered me to accompany him aboard the ship in the duty of security guard. I had already placed myself under his orders as per instructions in the code of conduct of the space services.

"Commander Todd sealed the entrance port against any further intrusion while we were away from the post, placing security into the machines designed for that purpose at the entrance port.

"We then proceeded to emergency hatch four."

Grovich pointed to the screen and pressed the start button.

"This is a recording of what then transpired. It is coded and approved as evidence by the court."

The tape started, showing Evans opening the hatch. He reached out the open door to help Hoshito aboard, then pulled Rivera in through the hatch. Todd and Grovich ran up and the rest was shown as it happened, blood and all. When the sectape was over Grovich continued, "I took the two prisoners into the brig area and secured them there. We then went to Luna base. All else is in the records as read by this court."

The defense attorney asked only a couple of questions, but nothing changed.

Todd found the slip about the judge's mention that the old man had intervened and approached the bench. He placed the slip on the bench before the judges and said clearly, "Prosecution calls the Honorary Commander of the Space Fleet, Karel Thames Grimes!"

There was a dramatic pause. The spectators started to murmur among themselves.

"Call Commander K. T. Grimes!" the bailiff called.

"Commander Grimes!?" a judge called out.

There was no response. The bailiff stood to ask loudly, "Is Commander Grimes in the witness room?"

He wasn't present.

"He was served with a warrant!" Todd stormed. "I want him

here and I want him here right now! I demand you issue a warrant for his arrest on contempt charges! This is unconscionable! Since when is any two-bit politician above the law? I won't stand for this!"

"I'll cite you!" the judge snapped.

"I beg the court's pardon," Todd said contritely. "This is a serious matter. This is treason and espionage and should the president of all Terra herself receive a subpoena I would expect her to appear – without question. There is no excuse for failing to answer that subpoena!"

"I agree," the judge said. "The tribunal demands that Karel Thames Grimes be brought before this body immediately!"

Todd glanced to see Pwester wink at him.

They waited for almost an hour before the MP's returned to say Grimes had left the Terran sphere in a private ship during the preceding night.

"This is a matter that cannot and will not be tolerated!" the tribunal said. "This supports the treason charges over simple espionage charges. It is definitely treason for the commander to go AWOL while under subpoena. The judges unanimously decree that the only hope now for the lessening of charges against any of the remainder of the various defendants is in full cooperation with this court! Be advised, all who hear these words, that these charges are capital! The charges to this court are plain!

"Hear this and beware!

"Karel Thames Grimes is hereby declared to be under sentence of death! Any member of any of the services who locates him anywhere is under direct orders to perform the execution without hesitation. All members of the services are, as of this moment, declared under article nine section eleven to be officers of this court for the duration of this action!

"We further determine Senators Hoshito and Rivera to be implicated in direct treasonous acts. They are ordered to be executed at sunset this day. Prosecutor! Call the next witness!"

The whole thing fell apart as the others couldn't wait to implicate each other. It had all been a plot for the politicians to take over the military and to drain much of the funding to their own uses. The judges used computers in their decisions so, in reality, had little actual power to decide guilt or innocence. They could only set sentencing within the guidelines decided by the machines. Any time those machines couldn't reach a clear-cut decision sentencing was set by vote of the judges.

When the old man ran it was as much as an open admission of guilt to the machines. They had given a ninety seven point four percent chance he was guilty of treason, at best (The computers weren't programmed to give one hundred percent) – thus the most extreme sentence.

The judges lessened the sentences of the others to life at hard labor, then the press started a huge exposee that resulted in other charges against other politicians.

Todd was seated across the table from the new "old man." The senate had given in to public pressure and had at last given a military job to a military man. The political choice would leave a bad taste to the public that would take a long time to go away. It was shown that Grimes had built a place on an outpost planet over the period of six years which he had carefully prepared for any possible trouble over his crooked policies. He had been located and was killed as he challenged the police with beam weapons that were also obtained illegally.

"Well, Carl," Todd said. "It looks like it turned out for the best. You were ahead of me through most of this, weren't you?"

Pwester laughed. "There was a law passed many years ago to give the senate power over the military," Carl answered. "At the time there were all sorts of juntas and coups and other military takeovers all over the world. That was even before we had a world government. It served quite well at that time, but it was never designed or meant that any of these politicians would have that strong a control.

"It seems no matter what the politicians get their hands on becomes crooked very quickly. This was no different. Times have changed tremendously and the military shouldn't even be called military anymore. We're now the space services, and that's our function. This is a temporary fix is all and that's really very sad."

"Time will tell," Todd answered.

"Time tells," Carl agreed. "You promised to avenge Old Mike and you've damned well done that! In spades!

"I hear you have Tab McGrew in your crew now. I hand-picked that man for you. He's up through the ranks and makes very few mistakes. I think you can use a moderating influence like him.

"Have you spent any time with him yet? How was the training trip?"

"Interesting," Todd answered. "I'll send you the report. A couple of things will interest you, I think."

"Something we can talk about?" Carl asked.

"Well, Tab saved my life and – oh yes – we found a neutron mass moon."

"I'll be damned!" Pwester cried. "Can I choose 'em or can I choose 'em!?!"

Chapter seven

Things were really hectic for a few days as scandal after scandal rocked the senate and the old military establishment. Todd was interviewed everywhere he went. He soon was longing to be aboard "The First Attempt" and away from Earth, but knew the time was critical. If meaningful changes were to be made in the way the people on this planet acted the time was now. In a few weeks or months the old ways would be back in full force unless protections were thought of and added.

President Greta Krause was forced to declare the government in jeopardy and to declare rule by decree. Todd watched her on the television and wondered if she was sincere or if she was merely another clever politician.

Clever wasn't the thing to be in this day and age. It would get you by last month, but now was the time to realize that the careful, methodical coyote often made a meal of the clever fox.

Pwester was having the constant cup of coffee with him in his rooms. McGrew and Ella were there with him. Ella was the one who made the comparison of the fox and the coyote while McGrew, who was leaning back in an overstuffed chair with his hands behind his head and his feet on the low magazine table, watched a small spider spin a web on the overhead light fixture. He spoke as though to himself.

"A long long time ago my Papa used to say to beware of clever people because they'll always get themselves in trouble in the end. If you're with them, no matter how much they pretend to be your friend, they'll try to switch the trouble to you.

"Clever people are always on some kind of weird ego trip. They confuse cleverness with intelligence. They always think they're smarter than those around them. Think they're smart enough to trick or fool their way out of anything they do. Manipulative, he called them.

"Intelligent ain't as quick as clever usually, but it's surer. In the long run intelligence always wins, then the clever ones sit back and lick their wounds like a burned monkey wondering how it all happened. Never occurs to them it ain't smart to fool with a hot stove in the first place.

"Intelligent will figure out things and modify their actions to include what they can't change and that alone will often change things. Clever never stops trying to figure some angle, so nothing ever changes. People aren't...."

The phone buzzed and Todd picked it up.

"Commander Robert Todd?" a voice asked.

"Yes, who wants to know?" Todd asked.

"Please hold for a moment."

"No way!" Todd snapped. "I call you, I'll hold! You call me you'd better be ready to talk!"

He hung up.

"What was that about?" Pwester asked.

"Some idiot calls and says `please hold!'" Todd cried. "Where do these jerks get this? You don't call someone and put them on hold! What rock did that stupid broad crawl out from under?"

The phone buzzed again and Pwester grabbed it before Todd could reach it. He said, "okay" and grunted, then handed it to Todd, saying, "Don't hang up on the President of Terra again. It leaves a bad impression."

"Not half as bad as the one she left me with!" Todd snapped.

"That was just some bureaucrat secretary. Greta's not like that," Pwester admonished him.

Todd was going to ask how he knew her well enough that he called her by her first name, but he had the phone.

"Commander Todd?" the president's pleasant soft voice asked. "I ask that you please forgive my office for the rudeness of a moment ago. I spent months trying to train her how to act while using the telephone, then she takes a week's vacation and I have it all to do over again.

"Could I impose on you to ask you to come to the capitol for a meeting? Carl and your friends are invited, of course."

"Why, certainly!" Todd replied. "Please forgive my shortness with your secretary. I was raised to never do that and it gets me mad. I'm afraid the events of the last several days have me a bit on edge."

"You and everyone else!" she agreed wryly. "You and I are caught in the very middle and we're going to stay there.

"Could you come soon?"

"Half an hour?" Todd asked.

"That will be excellent!" she said. "I'll have someone waiting for your arrival at E gate on Independence Street."

They said their goodbyes and Todd turned to the others. "I'm to go to the capitol building right away. I'm to bring CARL and my friends, so you two try to make yourselves presentable. Please try to act like human beings for this once in your lives.

"On second thought, cancel that. Don't act like human beings. The disgusting way they've been acting lately is really rather nasty!"

"They act exactly like they always have," Ella pointed out, grinning. "We'll try to conduct ourselves as though we had a modicum of culture and proper upbringing.

"Carley-Warley, what's this between you and Grettie Wetta?"

Pwester was very red-faced. "That was all over years ago!" he said defensively.

"Whoa!" Tab cried. "Warning! Touchy area!"

Pwester grinned and said, "We ... dated a few years back."

"Dated?" Ella said, raising an eyebrow and sniffing.

"Okay, say we *lived* together for a couple of months! It didn't work out," Pwester replied. "It's none of your business! It's nobody's business!"

"There're still a lot of feelings there," Ella said. "You're overreacting. Horribly!"

"Look, just drop it, okay?" Pwester pleaded. "It's personal. We're good friends who have made it a point to avoid one another because it always gets too sticky. I really shouldn't go to this meeting, but that's personal and my job requires that I *do* attend when I'm needed."

"She's politics and you're science and they just don't blend well," Ella said. "I'm as ready to meet Earth's president as I'll ever be. Is she really as nice as she seems on telly, Carl?"

"Yes. She's honest and forthright, she has a wonderful sense of humor and she's absolutely qualified for the job," Pwester said. "She's truly concerned for people and she worries too much, but she can be as hard as TitCroPlat alloy when the occasion calls for it, I guarantee! She's certainly nobody's fool!

"Her air of `Good old Aunt Essy' is deceptive as all hell. She's a great speaker, but when her eyes get that dark greyish cast and she sets her teeth, watch out! She'll chew you up and spit you out all over the sidewalk!"

"You're still in love with her!" Ella declared. "She never married and you never married.

"We'll have to see what we can do about that!"

Tab groaned. "Just what we need! A busybody matchmaker while the whole world goes to hell in a hand basket!" he complained. "You women are all alike!"

"That's why you men can't live without us!" she said, grinning brightly.

"You'll stay out of Carl's private life, Ella, and we'll all try to act like we deserve our positions whether we really do or not," Todd said. "That's an order!"

"Yowser, Boss! Doan hit me no mo'! Ise'll be good, oh yowser Massuh!" Ella cried and giggled.

As they went out Todd had visions of the disaster he was sure this would turn into.

They were led from the E gate to a large conference room. When the President came in she nodded, smiled a tight little smile toward Pwester, then asked if they would feel more comfortable in a less formal setting. This was, after all, not really official business in an official sense if they could read between the lines.

Carl introduced everyone, then they adjourned to another room where there were comfortable chairs and a sofa, which Ella soon contrived to get Pwester and President Krause on together with a rather obvious ploy. Todd glared at her.

"I want to know where you go from here, Commander Todd," the President said. "I can see you wish to separate the military from the Space Services – and I agree. Have you considered that your own commission is military?"

"That can be restructured," Todd suggested. "Declare the Space Services to be a scientific endeavor, that you'll keep all those who are now part of Services. You can declare them automatically transferred to the services department. The military is to be reduced to a needed minimum department. You can cite the recent problems as automatically invoking presidential command. Article four ninety seven sections C and D. Old Mike and Carl put that little stinger in when we revised."

"You're much too young for your position," Krause said. "You have to realize that it isn't all nearly that simple. The politicians aren't going to allow that without a fight all the way. There will have to be a mechanism whereunder we can achieve the goal, but we must make it seem to be *their* idea."

"The politicians are under the greatest pressure right now," Pwester said. "We can utilize that to make it seem the only way to stop the corruption is to separate the two problem departments."

"The only way we can constitutionally have a Space Services under government is defense – and that's military," Krause said.

"Madame President, if I might make a little suggestion?" Tab asked.

"That's what we're here for – and I'm called Greta, not Madame Anything. This isn't formal. May I call you Tab and Robert and Ella?"

"Everybody calls me Todd," Todd said. "I think we can be on a first name basis here, but we have to remember in other types of situations that we're speaking to and of the President and temper our remarks accordingly."

"If we're in a formal situation we'll act formally. Agreed," Greta said. "What's your suggestion, Tab?"

"You can publicly express your total outrage at the depths to which the offices of government have recently and publicly sunk and call an immediate constitutional convention to update the document. Wave a clause before the people that makes transgressions of this magnitude automatic treason with a required capital sentence. Say that the dire consequences of modern-day technology make it as much as imperative that the constitution be broadened to include that.

"Establish a Department of the Sciences or something on that order, then make government-funded research and exploration automatically come under that department, the head to be chosen like the supreme court – nomination by the president from a list supplied by the full cabinet with approval by two thirds or three quarters or whatever of the senate.

"You could have, say, three people to head the board, each appointed for ten or twelve years. You can then appoint Carl and a few other people you can trust to the first board and put Space Services under the department's aegis because it's basically an exploratory arm of the government, anyhow.

"The people'll ratify it so fast you won't believe it and the senate won't dare refuse Carl for the first Chief Scientific Administrator.

"You can wait until your next term to note that the military is mostly a research organization so IT should be under that department, too! You could do all of that by decree.

"Full circle!"

"Carl, where did you find this jewel?!" Greta asked. "It could work if we presented it properly. It wouldn't be subterfuge to express outrage. I'm certainly filled to overflowing with that! I have been for some time, but my hands have been effectively tied.

"I like the treason thing, but how can we word it?"

"Just state in preamble that perjury is treason in an elected official. They each took an oath to follow the constitution. Not doing so makes their oath perjury," Todd said. "The courts can't argue with that. They wouldn't dare under present circumstances."

Greta looked thoughtful for a few minutes, then grinned. They talked awhile, then the meeting broke up. Carl stayed to have dinner with Greta. Ella had a smug and satisfied look on her face as the others said their goodnights, then went their separate ways.

"...cannot, I repeat, can *not*, continue this senseless and unproductive charade!" President Krause was saying.

The group, Carl Pwester, Tab McGrew, Ella Forbes and Todd were watching the first public announcement of the constitutional convention.

"Therefore, it has become incumbent upon this government to change the system's flaws in any way we can to eliminate the possibility of this corruption ever happening again. I am outraged, as each and every citizen of this world should be that those entrusted by the public to carry out their wishes would so defiantly and so, damn it! – so dishonestly! – try to directly contravene the very essence of all those things we have for so long held sacred!"

She was a superb speaker. She leaned toward the camera and looked directly deeply into the audience's eyes.

"I am sick and tired of all the flowery phrasings and all the `statesman' crap!" she confided conspirationally. "I am sick and tired of being jerked around by a bunch of self-serving crooks! That's all they are!

"The constitution very plainly gives us a way out of this. The founders knew full well that the types who retained any great power for too long would become corrupt. They foresaw the need for us to *do something* about it.

"I definitely intend to do something about it!

"Are you with me?"

In their mind's eye (or ear) they could plainly hear the millions cheering.

Greta leaned back, smirked at the camera, then winked. "Yeah!" she exclaimed. "They gave us a way to handle this situation! Oh, yes! They did! They saw this coming!

"I am not going to waste my time trying to get the very ones who must be stopped short to act on this. I take it directly to you, the people who are affected. "Let this be fair warning, more than those slimeballs ever gave any of us, that Old Aunt Essy has just decided to become Matilda the Hun where those crooks are concerned! I'm going to run roughshod over your treasonous butts, so you'd be smart to get your treasonous butts out of my way!

"I say treasonous and I mean treasonous! You have each and every one taken an oath before God and the people to uphold and defend the constitution, yet you have each and every one twisted and attacked the constitution.

"No more!

"You have allowed and even encouraged the military to become, not a defense organization, but a contentious, obstructive, unbelievably greedy, totally corrupt, belligerent against the Goombridgians, who do not themselves want trouble.

"The military cannot hope to hold such power over the people of Earth without an enemy so they invented that supposed enemy. Goombridge fifteen eighteen is eleven lightyears from here! How in hell can one wage war at that distance? Can't you see we are NOT fooled?

"Listen to me! Listen closely and remember, then go to the polling places next Tuesday and vote YES! For amendments one and two.

"Amendment one states: Every elected member of government shall be required to take or to refuse the oath of office. That oath plainly states the member's promise to uphold and to defend the constitution above all other things. Should the swearing of that oath be refused that person shall not be seated.

"Those who take the oath place themselves in jeopardy of trial on a charge of treason against the people should they dare to break that oath, as the breaking of word oath is legally defined as perjury.

"Perjury to the people is treason.

"The penalty for treason against the people shall be death!

"I mentioned Amendment two, people. We all know this situation has arisen solely because when the constitution was originally drawn up the founders had a far less expansive technology than we have today. They left the mechanism for us to include changes in the way the world runs as part and parcel of a mechanism that changes the constitution and its provisions.

"So! Amendment two will state: There shall then be a Department of the Sciences, which will be administered by a tribunal who will be appointed through direct nomination of the offices of the President and approved and confirmed by majority vote of the senate.

"Each officer, the Administrator of Sciences, the Secretary of Sciences and the Overseer of Sciences will be emplaced for a period of ten years or until voluntary retirement or termination through charges as stated under the Judiciary Review section, whichever comes first.

"All research and exploration shall be under the aegis of this office.

"This is the first time since its inception one hundred seven years ago that the Constitution of the Terran World Empire has been changed, but it is time!

"Help me throw these bums out! Vote on next Tuesday! Yes and yes for the amendments! I need two thirds vote! This is for you, me and the Terran World Empire! It is for your children and our grandchildren! You can make a difference! You *will* make a very great difference!"

The cameras faded out with Greta standing waving a clenched fist with the two fingers sticking out in the ages-old "V" for Victory sign.

"Very impressive woman," Tab said.

"We all are if you give us a chance!" Ella said. "She's sexy, too! Say what you like, it's an asset!"

"Wiggle your ass and wink a coy little bit and change the constitution?" Tab asked, grinning at her.

"It couldn't hurt!" she fired back. "Well? Carl, you should go to her to help with the pressures those crooks will throw at her. I wouldn't be at all surprised at assassination attempts, so be armed.

"Todd, you have to get the ship ready for the trip out next week. It might be a good idea for us to be away when Carl's put in office.

"Tab, you and I will get the ship supplied, then we'll get in touch with Nat on the Ecstasy. Can you take your scout out to her? Got the range?"

"I can take out some of the equipment. I'll put two more power units in before I go. I'll make it okay," he said. "Who made you commander?"

"One must seize an opportunity where and when one can!" she replied. "Fearless leader is daydreaming!

"Wake up, Kid!"

Todd grinned. "I'm waiting for you to screw up so I can bust you to private and get you off my ship!" he declared.

"I'll take my picture collection with me and you'll wish you were never born!" she fired back. "The ones with those baggy shorts with the little red foxes on them will be a scream!"

"I don't have any baggy shorts with anything on them!" Todd said.

"I know," Ella shot back. "I drew them on so the pictures wouldn't be too funny!"

When would he learn not to challenge her?

They joked a few minutes but knew she was right, so they went their separate ways.

For four days there was a lot of public debate and even direct threats from two senators whose homes were stormed and burned to the ground and who barely escaped with their lives. They went into hiding. The people were very definitely getting fed up with their crooked politicians.

Would there really be change here? In Todd's lifetime?

At the end of the four days Todd and Ella, along with the crew of "The First Attempt", went to Luna Base to check out the ship and to prepare for the expedition. They stayed until they had all voted on the amendments on Tuesday Earth Standard, then watched the returns on and off for the twenty four hours they came in.

Todd expected a unanimous vote for the changes and was very surprised it had only a sixty nine point four percent passage vote. The amendments were law, but he couldn't understand how anyone could vote against it.

"Because people are contrary animals and some will vote just to be `agin' something," Ella warned. "I'm surprised it passed on the first vote. I predicted it for the third vote.

"I've got an idea when we return in a couple of months things will really be a mess. Those politicians won't roll over and play dead. They have something evil up their collective sleeve. Bet on it!"

The following day, when they would have left, Tab wasn't

back yet so they delayed three more days, Greta announced the nominations for the Department of Sciences control. It immediately became very plain what the politicians would try to do. They were planning to refuse all placed nominations until someone was selected who they could control. One and a half million people surrounded the senate building the next morning demanding immediate confirmation. The senate called out the military, but Greta said that calling them for emergencies was the job of the president, not the senate and if they came she would declare the entire senate outlaw and the leaders of the military outlaw at the same time.

The military began mobilizing for a coup so Todd called Greta and Carl to say he wanted to pull an enormous bluff, but needed her authorization. She said he had it. She knew he wouldn't do anything too dangerous, meanwhile the situation was deteriorating by the minute so anything might help.

A starship is an awesome thing. No one down there knew they had dumped all their nuclear weapons, but everyone knew they had the beam weapons referred to as `asteroid voiders' – that could blast a cubic mile of solid rock to rubble and gravel in the blink of an eye. Todd linked with the worldwide satellite system and came on-camera.

"Leaders of the mutinying military moving on Capital City and Government Cities, hear this!" he announced. "This is the Robert Cole Todd, Commander of the starship "The First Attempt" in orbit above Earth, soon to be joined with the starship "Ecstasy".

"You know the awesome power of the weapons we carry.

"You have been given clear orders by your Commander in Chief, the President of the Terran World Empire, to not intervene into a political situation. To refuse orders is mutiny. Mutiny is no less treason than the actions of those whose orders you plot to follow. The penalty for treason is death!

"Peoples of Earth, go to your shelters. If the military moves one single step further against the direct orders of their

Commander in Chief this ship will destroy every treasonous one of them. There will be no further warnings."

Less than ten minutes later Greta came on to announce she had taken hard steps against the mutineers, as all had heard, and that a list of nine officers would be held and tried for treason as would each of the senators who had released the illegal orders to the military.

"Sooner or later if any of them survive they will learn the people of Earth mean business this time! ENOUGH!" she shouted, and held up the clenched fist with the victory sign. This time the broadcast played the sounds of the millions cheering.

From their place in orbit they watched through the large scopes as the military quickly withdrew.

"Someday someone's going to call one of your bluffs," Ella warned. "Then what?"

"Oh, I would've used the beam in tight focus on the HQ building," Todd answered. "They wouldn't have pushed anymore."

The following day Greta's choices were all confirmed and Tab and his Manta returned. They would finally begin their trip.

"I think we gave them pause for thought!" Todd said.

"Then you don't know politicians very well," Tab said, having just heard the explanations of what had happened while he was away. "This is a minor setback to them. They'll make what they call `contingency plans' and will proceed as always."

"If Greta will have the guts to execute those senators and generals now in custody it'll help a lot," Ella said.

"Oh, she'll do that!" Tab agreed. "It'll only drive them more underground.

"Remember, you got this far with patience. You aren't the only one who can play that game."

The following day they started their trip.

Chapter eight

Todd rendezvoused with the "Ecstasy" before continuing on toward his area of exploration to discuss the expected revisions in the way Space Services would be managed in the future. Todd managed to spend a little time with Natalie and they arranged to meet after the call-in that would come as soon as Carl Pwester had set up the new rules.

The "Ecstasy" was due for overhaul after the third ship in the services, "Solidarity", named after some old labor movement in the EuroTerran Sector of Earth. That meant three months from the present.

"I hope that the Terran political situation has stabilized better by then," Natalie said. "The last thing I need is a lot of hassle after being out here away from that sort of thing.

"I tell you true, Todd! I sometimes wish I could stay out here and forget that Earth even exists!

"Most spacers feel that way, I guess."

"The Mars Colony is almost ready to put the Deimos Base on line by the end of the year," Todd replied. "We've finished our overhaul, which is why we got tangled in that mess on Terra."

"From the tapes and mediafax Tab brought us I'd say it was you who started the mess!" she laughed. "McGrew is somebody I wish I could steal from you! Maybe Carl will make rules where we can hire away from each other. If he does Tab's gone. It really takes some guts to jockey a Manta scout way the hell out here. Eighteen lightyears!

"I know. Don't say it. I flew Mantas – still do – and trust them more than I do these big jobs. It's purely jealousy!

"He tells me Carl and Greta used to have a thing. Even lived together. I can believe what he said about Ella getting them back together again. I'll never forget her, either. She's number two I'll steal from you. Tatsumi, our medoff, is about as much fun as running out of oxygen outside in a suit.

"I don't know what's the matter with me! I'm chattering like a fool!"

"We have some catching up to do," Todd said. "Did Tab tell you about the neutron moon?"

"The whole service already knows about that!" Natalie exclaimed. "So help me, I'm beginning to believe in ESP. Do you know, it must have been no more than a couple of hours after you found it that the word that you had made a big find was going through this ship like an ion storm? – And we were a good thirty lightyears from you."

"I'll never understand how that works," Todd replied. "Old Mike told me he was on the Tau Ceti expedition when M'tai bought it clear over by Ross one fifty four. It wasn't more than a gut feeling, but they all became saddened. He didn't know why, but everyone *knew* something was wrong and they knew it was that ship where whatever it was happened. I guess ESP works in some other plane because nothing moves that fast in this one."

"I think it proves they will someday have instantaneous radio or something such," Natalie agreed. "If thought travels that fast other things can.

"How did we get on this?"

"We're grasping for reasons to not have to say goodbye," Todd answered. "I don't want to leave and I think you don't want me to leave. I have to admit I found myself attracted to you from the first meeting at your scout. I'd sworn to avenge Old Mike's murder so had to forego saying anything then. I've done that and can say it now.

"I don't believe how hard it is to say something so simple and true!"

"My god!" Natalie exclaimed. "What do you mean `Old Mike's murder?' I thought he had a heart attack!"

"There was nothing wrong with his heart," Todd said. "He had it checked regularly and would have been grounded years before if that was even a possibility. No commander can have even a normal standard arrhythmia that's found in ninety percent of the people. You know that. Just look at what Ella or Mr. Moto or whoever puts you through before every trip you take!

"He was assassinated by Grimes, or by Grimes' orders. I took care of Grimes!"

"They found Grimes at Tau Ceti trying to con those strange people into protecting him," Natalie said. "Guy by the name of Ellis, old friend on some outpost planet found him. The Taus said it was none of their business so he would have to handle things he brought on himself by himself.

"Ellis marched up to him on the street and said, `Mike Cogsworth was my friend and was worth a million like you,' then reached out and cut his throat with a dull hunting knife.

"I hear the Taus sentenced him to cleaning the sidewalk where Grimes bled and that was that. They don't think anything about murder because they say murder is a family matter.

"I think they're right. In this case, anyhow."

Todd grinned and agreed. "I guess we're really pretty barbaric as a race, but the Taus are socially advanced over us. They look like octopuses – octopi? – but I like them. Have you ever met any of them?"

"No, just pictures," she said. "They look so strange! I hear they think in a very different way than we do. The translators are theirs. Their technology is way above ours. They travel in our ships sometimes and in the Goombridgian ships at times and tell us both we're stupid to make warlike noises at one another.

"Ella is standing at the door giving you a dirty look!"

"Yes, Colonel Forbes?" Todd asked.

"Tell her you love her, make arrangements for the wedding and let's get the hell out of here!" Ella said, getting a deep blush from Todd.

"I tried to pass over his statement of attraction," Natalie confided. "I like him too, but I'm a spaceship commander so we simply won't have the time to be together for awhile yet. In two years I intend to look him up!"

Todd laughed and said, "That's all I could ask! I know you'll be there in two years so I'll wait for you!"

They soon left with Todd on a cloud. Even Ella's little barbs didn't bother him. Then they were on their way to a new area for a new system exploration. Todd met his crew, then went with the pilots to the outship bay to examine their craft as carefully as they always did before any flight. There was sabotage to three of the craft. It was all exterior damage, as no one could enter the keyed portals except the pilots. The damage probably wouldn't have been detected had the inspections not been so very minute.

Todd called all the pilots together. "This was done at Luna Base within two days of liftoff," Todd said. "That's why Tab's Manta wasn't hurt. He was out here on a secret mission for Gretta and the Terran government."

"It was done by a military-trained man and was to get you," Tab said.

"How do you figure?" Todd asked.

"They have someone else to inspect the ships, exteriors are cursory in the military," Tab said. "There was no reason to go after anyone else. They didn't know our system, they damaged all three ships so as to get the one they were after.

"It was political. They knew the shield and how it works in TTH planes. With the grid out of sync like that you would go into TTH and never come out again.

"Question is, what do we do about it?"

"We repair the damage and act as though nothing has happened, do a single survey run, find an excuse and go back to Luna Base," Todd suggested. "Then I show you how Old Mike showed me a few things about the military and why the system's so stupid.

"Run every least test you can think of before jumping the bay, then think up a few new ones. I want to set up a spy camera system to record the expression on every single person's face we see at Luna Base as we come down the ramp. I want reactions and I want them plain!"

He called the radio/com man, Kim, and had him start arranging video cameras on zoom lenses – all they had, and they had plenty.

The pilots worked together, were able to install new grids and to check all circuits on all four scouts in three days, then they made their surveys, finding two usable planets and a lot of rocks and ice. One was an "X"ed lifeform planet.

Ella had become a regular member of the special group and Kim was invited to join. Tab was in, as was Todd. They met in Todd's cabin, which was roomiest as it had an office built in for the commander to use, though all the cabins were roomy if efficient. You couldn't ask people to spend a year at a time in space and over-confine the space they had for privacy.

The meetings were casual. Many plans were thought of, laughed at and thrown out. Todd would grin and say he would handle the Luna Base part and would find who had done the actual sabotage work, but they would have to find the connection between the ones who did the dirty work and the ones who gave the orders.

"I want to be able to hand the schemers over to the senate, who'll have a fullscale revolt on their hands if they don't find them guilty of treason. Seems they've sabotaged their own world's defense ships!"

"Uh-uh! They aren't defense ships anymore," Ella pointed out. "We were able to cut the military out, remember?"

"True, but not at the time the sabotage was performed!" Todd cried, laughing. "One day later and they would have been science survey ships, but the last day they could have done it was the morning of the day we took off to back up

Greta. That session was the one that made the revisions into law.

"I was trained in law for the prosecution of the Grimes case, as they call it now, though *that* was an espionage and treason trial. I *know* that law backwards, forwards, in, out and from any side. They've really played right into our hands with this. If they have any public support now they sure as hell won't have it soon.

"If Greta's having any trouble with that senate she can call elections over this. Maybe I can really see a change in my own lifetime. I didn't dare to hope that would ever happen!"

"Ella, I want you to carry your medical bag everywhere and I want a `strange band' radio set in that bag. Kim can build one that only he can receive in this ship. He'll have the complete computer setup ready and will give and take information over the radio circuit.

"We're going to have to move fast when we land. I think we have to have this done in no more than a couple of hours – and we might have to play a little bit dirty ourselves. Sometimes it's necessary to start a backfire to prevent the whole forest from burning.

"We should be on Luna Base in about six hours so let's get this together.

"Kim, how long to modify a handset with the power to reach anywhere on Luna?"

"They'll be ready before we get there," Kim promised and went out.

"Ella, carry the full technical analysis bag. Another little insignificant little machine won't be noticed among all that stuff," Todd said.

She nodded and went to pack a bag.

"Looks like we're committed – or should be," Tab said.

"We just might be before this is over," Todd replied.

"The First Attempt" settled majestically onto the "locker pad," then moved on the tracks into the dome at Luna Base.

The massive section slid closed and the atmospheric tube moved up to automatically attach itself to the lower port at the same time as the "pad" lowered the ship onto its cradle. The port cycled open as soon as the pressure was correct in the tunnel. The ramp slid into its socket inside of the tube.

There were eight or ten people in the tunnel waiting for the crew to disembark. What they saw first was a large plastene one-way carrier globe (Light would go in, but none came out. The reverse of the standard package) lowered on a cargo pallet. What they *didn't* know was it contained a series of video cameras to watch them.

Next came Ella with a grim look on her face, then Kim stood to glare over the people from the top of the ramp. He soon went back inside, then several of the survey crew came down the ramp. They had strict orders to avoid speaking or signaling in any way to anyone there.

Then came the pilots, laughing and joking among themselves, Tab loudly saying, "...that, my dear, is how a torpedo works!" The four pilots laughed boisterously, the sounds ringing and bouncing around the tunnel.

As they passed on through, looking as though they had no idea anyone else was in the tunnel, Todd was saying, "There were these two women in the Bronx who met on a street corner one day, Lola and Bridgette. Well, Lola says, `Hey, Bridgie! You seem rather in a state! Whatever is the matter?' and Bridgette replies ...."

As they passed on down the tube Todd noticed two men in ship maintenance uniforms who were staring at them as if they were seeing ghosts. He waved his hand around as if it were part of the joke, pointing in their direction for the smallest instant before they moved on. Kim would zoom the video to read their tags and would make closeup singles of each of them. He was doing that with everyone, but Todd wanted to catch their expressions.

The four split into two groups of two, Lisa Zume and Karel

Moska would go to the maintenance and repair depot where they were to order several types of replacement parts while listening to the gossip. The parts they wanted would take a little time to gather and they would want to "inspect" each item, claiming they needed new ones because the ones on the ship, ordered through this very facility, were faulty. (They had intentionally damaged a number of parts by putting current through the wrong direction or removing a connector wire.)

Todd and Tab strolled into the debriefing room where Colonel Sanchez was talking to three other officers. Ella was sitting well to the side behind a phony palm in a pot. She winked at them and smirked.

Todd noticed Sanchez because as he and Tab came into the room Sanchez's hand jerked, spilling a cup of scalding-hot coffee all over the front of his uniform. The others turned to see Todd and Tab and looked puzzled. Todd greeted them and said, "You should be more careful, Colonel Sanchez. One could get burned very badly doing things like that!"

He went to the table to drop the tapes of their survey into the receptacle. Tab sat, leaned back, then stood to go to the service table where he got himself a cup of coffee. Sanchez was looking nervous as he returned to sit at the table. Todd took his own maps and papers from the briefcase he carried, put his data recorder on the table beside them, got his own coffee and turned to call Ella to come on over with the med reports. When Ella came out from behind the palm Sanchez started sweating visibly. He was stammering a bit as he dismissed the people he was talking to. He came slowly over to the debrief desk. He had a very sick smile on his face as he nodded at them and sat in his chair.

"Why, Colonel Sanchez!" Ella cried, looking at him in alarm. "You're ill! Whatever is the matter with you?"

He waved a hand and said that it was nothing. Something he ate.

"Nonsense!" Ella cried. "Here! Botulism can be fatal. Here. Let me monitor you. Should I call the infirmary?"

"No, no! It's nothing!" he snapped. "Leave me alone!"

"Now-now. Just let me put the blood pressure and electrical response and this little ek/eg hookup on. You won't even notice it. It'll let us know if you're poisoned or that you're overworked and over stressed," she chided.

"Colonel Forbes! Leave it! That's an order!" Sanchez cried.

"As a full commander, I order you to allow the health monitoring," Todd said. "We can't have a sick man running this section!"

Sanchez set his jaw and glared at Ella, who blithely ignored him, pressed the four buttons to him and turned on her machines in her case.

"Isn't that better?" she asked.

"Colonel Sanchez," Tab said. "There was sabotage to the scouts on "The First Attempt". That sabotage was done here on Luna Base while my Manta wasn't aboard, so it occurred on the day or night before the ship lifted to duty for the president. What do you know about that?"

"Me!? Nothing!" Sanchez cried.

"Who do you work for?" Todd asked. "I mean, which one set that sabotage up and why?"

"This...! This is outrageous!" Sanchez yelled. "What are you accusing me of? What right do you have to assume I had anything to do with those grids? I demand an apology!"

"Colonel Sanchez," Tab stated dryly. "You're attached to a machine that measures pulse rate, blood pressure, electrical skin variations, EKG and ECG information and nervous tension. Almost a hundred years ago that was called a lie detector. They weren't accurate then and quite a lot of people were wrongfully accused because of them, so they were finally thrown out. We've improved them a thousandfold now. They're accurate.

"You're a baldfaced liar! We'll find who was behind this and we'll fry their asses and yours along with them! Your only hope is to come clean."

"You have nothing! You have no proof and no evidence! This is an outrage!" Sanchez cried, pulling off the electrodes.

"Hmm? Then how did you know it was the grids that were sabotaged?" Todd purred. "Lucky guess?"

"Well, that is I merely assumed that you...." Sanchez stammered. "I don't have to answer your questions! This is all fictitious! I demand an apology!"

"Nope! I'm a full commander and you *will* answer my questions!" Todd snapped. "Either here or at your trial for treason! You know full well the law on treason and I'll personally handle your execution for attacking my people on my ship! Do I make myself quite clear?"

"You have no authority to question me and we both know it!" Sanchez replied. "You can talk with my lawyer about that! I'm here to debrief the mission and I don't know what you're talking about!

"Sabotage? On Luna Base? Impossible!"

"Very well," Todd said and waved Tab to sit. Tab was preparing to wring Sanchez's neck for him. "I'll have to bring the charges against you for treason, then.

"The information is all recorded from the survey. If there are no further questions now I'm sure you'll want to meet with your lawyer. You're going to need him. You'll need a bunch of them, but you're a walking dead man.

"Come on, guys. Let's see what the others have come up with."

They picked up their stuff and walked out to return to the ship's communications room where Kim had recorded the entire proceeding in the debriefing room – including the readouts from Ella's machines.

"We can be sure the two maintenance men out there, numbers two fourteen five thirty seven and five sixty two, Lon Lossiter and Sarah Meier, are the two who did the actual sabotage, but I'm as sure they were working under direct orders from Sanchez," Kim said. "Is that how you read it?"

"Yes," Todd said. "What we've got to keep foremost in mind is that they're all part of something originating in the senate. Sanchez and these two are part, but not even a large part of it all."

"The politicians are trying to get control of Space Services again. That means you and Pwester must die," Ella said. "That means in its turn that the military is striking out to get the ships back under their control, are manipulating the senate and are running this whole mess."

"I agree," Tab said. "You made one mistake when you announced to the world that you have the means to wipe out their army if they interfered with the public and with the senate proceedings. That really brought home to them that their only power advantage is in the large ships. Now that they no longer have any control of the large ships they have no advantage whatever – and they know it. That makes them far more dangerous."

"They'll do anything in their power to retain any control they can, including killing us all off and killing off half the senate as well. They won't protect their own. We have to get in touch with Carl and Greta right now! They must have protection!" Ella demanded.

"They'd like to knock President Krause off, too," Kim agreed. "I have the line you asked tapped, Todd. My meter says it's in use."

They went to the radio room and turned on the recorder to hear gobbledegook.

"It's coded. I don't have the key," Kim said.

"Oh, for...!" Todd said. "I didn't think they'd code on what they think is a secure frequency!

"Now what?"

Kim grinned. "How 'bout if a bottle servo were to sorta accidentally carry a little bug right into Sanchez's office?" he asked.

Ella grinned and asked, "How can you get it close enough to the set to hear them?"

"I'm going to use a bit of inductance from the preamp before it gets to the coder," Kim said. "They call them bottle servos for a good reason. They look like bottles. I'll paint one to look like it should be there. They have all these phony plants sitting around so they'll get another one. I'm sure this message will be answered later. It's four thirty A.M. in Government Cities now so they'll have to get someone out of bed.

"You have to get Sanchez out of the office for five minutes. That's all. It doesn't matter if he locks. There isn't a lock in this system I can't open. They're all electronically keyed so I can identify and rematch with a residual recorder. I guarantee I can open any one of them in less than thirty seconds."

Todd grinned. "Tab, get him out of that office in exactly ten minutes from now. Kim, be there and be ready.

"Ella, you and I will make ourselves obvious in the cafeteria where we'll be seen by one and all.

"It's time to meet with Lisa and Karel. Maybe they've come up with something else for us to work on from another angle.

"How will you handle it, Tab?"

"I'll call him, tell him that he's going to explain a little something to me in person about this crap in the briefing room right now or I'll go public. I'll tell him I have a reporter on standby.

"He must grab what time he can, so he'll come running as fast as he can. If he doesn't shut me up before he gets advice from his friends all hell will drop on them all. They're afraid of the public now so they're terrified of the press. We're important basically because we can bring the people down on them before they can get away."

Tab went to the interphone, punched Sanchez's code, snapped out a few quick sentences into the mouthpiece, said he would be in the briefing room in five minutes – and would see a reporter in six if Sanchez wasn't there. He turned and said, "Let's get it on!"

"Tab, go armed. Stand to the side so if they do try anything stupid – more than usual, that is – you won't be in the line of fire. I won't be at all surprised if he tries to knock you off on general principles," Todd said.

"I sort of figured they might so I'm prepared," Tab replied. "I have a reflective panel sewed into this uniform. They'd use a laser in those quarters, we can be sure. I'll have to protect my head. No shield there."

"No danger!" Ella quipped. "No mere cutting laser could affect anything that hard!"

They grinned, saluted and went to their duties.

<u>Chapter nine</u>

Todd and Ella went to the cafeteria, spoke with a few people they knew, then strolled casually into records where Todd had the man on duty call up the past records of "The First Attempt". He sat at a desk screen to study them, mumbling into Ella's bag that information he felt was pertinent. They then strolled around the base facilities for awhile before returning to the ship. Tab greeted them and grinned. He was sitting with his feet on Kim's desk while Kim listened with earphones to a small homemade set.

"This is the fourth call he's gotten on that secure set," Tab said. "Senators Kirsch and Karpov and now Kirsch again.

"Did you find anything?"

"Yes. We confirmed that our two maintenance people had access to the ship," Todd replied. "Little bits and pieces we can use to build a solid case."

Kim giggled and put the earphones across the set.

"Sanchez just informed the good Senator Kirsch that he was an idiot to think he could possibly hear from The General, whoever that may be, while a bunch of political asses were tying up the frequency," Kim said. "You'd think they'd know that!"

"How good is your tie-in?" Ella asked.

"There's a bottle of artificial daisies and ferns about this high sitting right on top of the set, Kim said. "I hear every word – both ways."

"Ferns with daisies?" Ella said. "How ghastly!"

"*And* irises! I know," Kim said. "No one in their right mind would make an arrangement like that one so it must belong there! It *is* typical of that kind of thing."

Ella said, "Ain't it the truth! Did you see that gaudy thing with orchids and daylilies in the foyer? Have you ever seen anything so tasteless in your life?"

Page 123

"Excuse me, but did we come here to critique the flower arrangement in the foyer or to catch some saboteurs?" Todd asked.

"To criticize flower arrangements, of course!" Ella said. "We *know* who the spies are!"

"I say five bucks on General Levant," Tab said.

"You got it!" Kim shot back. "I say five on General B. Arnold L. Schmidt!"

"You're both on!" Ella cried. "I say it's Fatso Brooks!"

"You're all on, and I say General D'Angona," Todd put in. "That'll be the easiest fifteen I've picked up in a long time!"

"Okay, bets are down," Ella agreed. "Why D'Angona?"

"Because Sanchez went through high school with him. He was D'Angona's aide until the Space Service broke away from Military Branch – and I've always wondered how Sanchez got a commission in Services. His tongue is an inch thick in boot polish!" Todd said. "That's why I know I'll take these bets. You each took someone you dislike personally. You've got to be logical – like me! I dislike all of 'em!"

The light came on and Kim put on the earphones. He listened for a few minutes, then hung up.

"Great logic, boss!" he announced. "What do we do if nobody guessed?"

"Who was it?" Tab asked.

"Ledderer, retired," Kim answered. "He owns a munitions plant. Sponsored both Sanchez and D'Angona. Been in the news with that `we've got to be prepared for the worst from Goombridge!' line."

"Let's hear it," Todd suggested.

Kim ran the tape back and put another cassette in the recorder while they listened to that one.

"Here goes," Kim said.

There was a pause, then, "... while you damned idiots keep the channel blocked with a bunch of stupid asinine questions!" a much longer pause, "Sanchez?"

"Yes? General?"

"What the hell have you screwed up now?"

"Mr ... uh, General Ledderer, the grid fault, er, you know, didn't get Todd. It didn't get anybody! That McGrew character says they've traced the saboteurs and they led them straight to me.

"What do I do now?"

"First thing, don't panic! Arrange an accident for the ones who did the work so there will be nothing they can use in any court against you. I should think that much would be obvious even to you."

"But, uh, sir! They're our people!" Sanchez exclaimed.

"Damn it, you sniveling wimp! They knew the risks! Use your head! They already fingered *you*! Don't argue with logic, just do it! And don't call me anymore. I can't afford the risk. Don't call Kirsch again, either. He's a fool! Don't call Karpov, he runs his mouth too much. Use the D'Angona connection, but be careful. He's a coward and will spill his guts if they question him the right way. These family men are a weak link! Too easy to pressure!

"Keep me out of it. Is that clear?"

"Yes, uh, yessir," Sanchez replied.

Then silence.

"You know the risks. Work for *me* and I'll have you shot if you get caught," Ella said. "Better order protective custody for Lossiter and Meier.

"I wonder what that will bring out?"

"We'll play that tape for them. Maybe they'll open up a bit," Tab suggested. "We can't have them held here. Sanchez can get them too easily."

"Get them aboard the "Attempt" right away. We'll play the tape for their education," Todd said. "The rest will be their choice.

"Tab, let's you and me take my Manta to visit our CO and the president, shall we?

"Make us a copy of the tape, Kim. Ella, you get Lossiter and Meier aboard and handle things here with Kim. You're to be in charge until I return. Make a medical emergency form to bring them in. You have the authority to order that, but do it fast!

"Ready, Tab?"

"Yo!" Tab said and stood. "I can use some planetside. I'd like to tour Mars Colony while we have the Manta out anyhow."

They went to the "bottom," took the scout out and headed for Earth. They used a private channel to the president from orbit and were given a special landing spot on the vacation island.

"We can protect this place, so Carl and I have been running things from here," Gretta said. "What's it about?"

"Oh, a few things have come up," Tab replied. "Mainly just a visit. You already have a full report on the attempted sabotage. Sanchez was behind it, but we can't prove anything. Maybe you could bust him as Commander in Chief and get him out of there?"

"Done!" she said. "I'll have Carl do it, though. They're not military anymore so he can claim incompetence. If Sanchez makes a stink we'll bring him to trial. Maybe we can't convict him, but we can ruin his name and that would do as well.

"See you in half an hour!"

"What was that all about?" Todd asked. "It's a secure channel. They can't intercept."

"Like the one in Sanchez's office?" Tab asked.

"Touche'!" Todd returned.

They landed and went in to be greeted by Carl and Gretta and twenty others so had to play the diplomatic game for awhile, then were finally alone with their friends.

"Okay, what's the real scoop?" Gretta asked. "You really gave some funny looks to Senator Karpov!"

"What is that traitor doing here on this island?" Tab asked carefully.

Carl registered shock and Gretta stood staring at him.

"I'd call you a few choice names if I weren't so sure you wouldn't say that without proof of some sort," Gretta said. "I always considered Karpov to be one of the more trustworthy people around here!"

"We'll play a tape for you," Todd said. "Maybe we can use him for our own purposes if we keep him unaware of what we know.

"We know that whatever we tell him will get back to Ledderer fast. Misinformation can be most useful."

"Ledderer?" Carl asked. "Isn't he some kind of arms dealer or something such? Wants us to arm against Goombridge?"

"He's also behind all of this," Tab said. "I figure he was the one who ordered the sabotage on our scouts."

"Did Kim give you the frequency?" Carl asked. "We'll trace it and get him with the goods, so to speak."

"Tab has it," Todd said. "Don't grab it or him until he gets the messages we want out.

"Tab, call the ship and use our personal code. Tell Ella and Kim not to grab Lossiter and Meier. That would give us away."

Tab headed to the Manta and was back in a few minutes. Todd had played the tapes of Sanchez's conversations for Gretta and Carl, who had quickly arranged sealed indictments by decree against all the participants. If anything went wrong they would still have to face a prosecutor. Carl had that power as Chief Administrator of Space Services while the president had no such power.

Tab returned to say the two maintenance people were just being brought aboard so Ella would check them for radiation poisoning and would call the other two maintenance people who had worked on the ship, saying they had discovered dust a defective servo had missed. Maybe the nervous tension would really make them sick.

"Okay, let's give Karpov some story," Gretta said. "He's very anxious to attend any briefings held with `our fabulous heroic science officers from the Services!' as he puts it."

"Then we should have a full debriefing this evening," Todd agreed. "We'll explain about the sabotage and will say dear old Sanchez, blah, blah, blah. Give them the rope to hang themselves."

They then talked of other things after Gretta called Karpov to say he could attend a general debriefing in two hours. They had a meal, then went into the conference room to find Karpov already there. They placed recorders and began.

"Commander Todd, please report to this committee the reasons you have called special session debriefing. You will also explain the necessity of having the president at this meeting," Carl said into the microphone.

Todd stood. "Madame President, Admiral and others, I bring before you charges most serious and of a nature that indicate that the president is in some danger.

"On our last survey trip we found that three of our four Manta class scout ships had serious and dangerous exterior grid damage. That damage was deliberate sabotage.

"May I ask if the gentleman attending as observer has full security clearance?"

"He does," Gretta said.

"I will continue," Todd said. "The sabotage was done on Luna Base within thirty six hours of our departure from that facility. There were but three scout ships aboard at takeoff and those three were all sabotaged. Captain Tab McGrew was on special mission and his scout was unharmed."

"On Luna Base?! No! A saboteur?!" Karpov shouted.

"Please do not interrupt, Senator," Carl said. "Proceed please Commander."

"We were able to repair the damage and, upon our early return, we checked all records. We were able to show that two maintenance people, and only those two, could have committed the sabotage.

"We were not able to get anything from them and do not have evidence strong enough to bring any charges, but we were also able to determine that only one person could have given them the orders to damage the ships. We therefore used a subterfuge on that person and determined he was indeed guilty.

"That evidence would be most doubtful in any court as it was obtained through the use of what was once called a lie detector, evidence that is inadmissible.

"This matter is most serious. It indicates an attempt by a person or persons to subvert the Space Services. No one but the now-weakened military could profit from such a move. That means an assassination or other form of coup, which means that Madame President is in danger.

"It is also obvious there is aid in high political offices to the traitors."

"Who is the perpetrator at Luna Base?" Pwester asked.

"Colonel Sanchez," Tab said. "We made him think we got our original information from Meier and Lossiter to put him on the lie detector through a subterfuge. I hope he doesn't find they said nothing – laughed in our faces as a matter of fact.

"I won't be all that sorry if Sanchez kills them! They tried to kill us!"

"Why would he kill them? And I've already instituted orders to remove Sanchez from office," Pwester said. "He's a total incompetent. I don't know *how* he got by me into that position, but we were in turmoil. As you say, there's someone in the senate who's neck deep in this, so that's how it was done."

"In the senate?!" Karpov cried. "Preposterous! I know those people! They wouldn't do such a thing!"

"They rather apparently *have* done such a thing," Gretta said. "We're faced with a partial fait accompli. Sanchez is in his high position and the sabotage was done. We'll have to find who it is. They're traitors and, totally regardless of any other factors, I'll see them executed to the last one! I'll personally give the `fire' order! I won't countenance a traitor!

"There's no longer the possibility of a traitor against any country or political unit. There's only a traitor against the human race.

"Captain McGrew, Commander Todd, this is a totally intolerable situation! I don't care that they would assassinate me, but I care deeply that they have managed to assassinate any qualities of decency and humanity they may have possessed.

"Do you have a strategy worked out with which to cope?"

"It isn't in a final form, Madame President," Todd said. "If we could meet with some security experts and some who are better skilled in discovering persons who are involved in such base criminal activity we should be able to formalize our conceptions and ideas."

"It will be done!" Gretta promised. "Tomorrow at ten hundred hours you and Captain McGrew will meet in this room with a group of people who will be selected and ordered to appear by myself and by Admiral Pwester. Please bring any notes or other items that may facilitate this investigation.

"I'll see you in the morning, gentlemen!"

Todd was awakened early by his talent of being able to tell himself before sleep that he wanted to awaken at a certain time and automatically doing so. He was up and around when Tab came into the room with the notes and tapes.

"We can set this up in some kind of order to make it go much smoother and faster," he said.

"Smoother and faster when?" Todd asked.

"At the meeting this morning," Tab replied.

"Are we actually going to have a meeting?" Todd asked.

"What?! Why not?" Tab cried.

"By now Karpov will have definitely proven his guilt," Todd answered. "There's no reason for a meeting. If we were to get a bunch of bureaucrats and politicians involved there would be a complete investigation, true, but it would take several years and all they'd want was someone to be the goat. Somebody like Sanchez, who's already caught, would be blamed for the whole thing. That would be that. Political investigations are all politics and no investigation. You know that."

"I'll say that Gretta had me convinced we'd have the meeting this morning," Tab said.

"She can't call these investigations, legally," Todd replied. "She can ask the judiciary to empanel one, but that takes time. Too much of it."

"What can she do, then? Why come to her at all except to see she protects herself?" Tab asked. "I'll tell you true, I don't know much about politics or the constitution. Exactly what powers does a president really have?"

"She has total access to the public," Todd said. "That's the important thing for a president. If he or she gets on worldwide media to explain what he or she sees must be done and doesn't get a response, then it probably wasn't deserved.

"President Borkins resigned when his fourth presentation to the public was rejected by them. All four were.

"You see, he made many promises as to what he would work for before the election and acted much differently after winning. The people wouldn't put up with that so no other president has tried that again. They all learned their lesson from that one.

"The constitution states that an elected official must vote as a majority of his constituency demands, so a president can appeal to the people, who write to the senators, who must be able to show proof they had their constituency's backing if called on to do so. Note the similarity between constitution and constituency!

"The old nations had their constitutions, but there was no force to guarantee the people's will would *ever* be followed so there was always trouble – even among those few who lasted past the first couple of public challenges.

"The big problem in this case is, though Gretta could definitely get the populace to demand action with a few speeches, we don't have time. We're talking about a coup attempt here."

Tab nodded. "I didn't want a lecture, but that will do nicely enough, thank you," he said. "We're working outside of the law. I don't mind that. What we have to do is what we have to do."

"We don't have to work outside of the law," Todd said. "Don't get me wrong – if we have to, we have to. I have no problem with that. I'm working for the safety of Space Services as well as for the people. I'm not some great statesman or any of that crap, but I'll damned well do anything I can to protect my people. That's simply what a commander's job requires."

"You're speechy as all get-out this morning, aren't you?" Tab asked. "What now?"

"Let's go see what Carl and Gretta have for us," Todd suggested.

They went to the breakfast room to find that Gretta was hard at work for more than an hour already, but Carl was there.

"He made the transmission and we've pinpointed the set. We put a bug in his room, so we have the whole thing from this end. You can hear some of the stuff from Ledderer, who did quite a lot of yelling because Karpov even called him. Karpov ended the thing by calling him some of the foulest names it's been my pleasure to ever hear! Fitting!" Carl said. "Haven't heard a word from him yet this morning, but I can imagine he'll attempt to force any investigation to go through the senate offices. He can do that. Mere presidents can't direct investigations. Got to get a court's permission. So does the senate.

"We'll see."

They waited awhile until Gretta came in. "I'm glad you're all here now. The tape's ready from when Karpov called Ledderer," she said with a grim look. "I expected to hear that we're not legally permitted investigations from Karpy by now.

"Damn! I hate this! I feel there isn't anyone in this whole world I can trust.

"We should go to the conference room and pretend we're having the meeting when Karpy comes in. We can listen to the tape there. It will be a reason to be there."

They went to the room and put the tape in the machine.

"Nobody but the operator has heard it yet. He says he told Carl about a few of the choicest names Karpy called Ledderer," Gretta explained.

She turned on the machine.

"click click scritch drone click."

"What's all that?" Tab asked.

"Only the standard noises in the room. The pickup is sound-operated," Carl answered.

There was the sound of a door opening, then a few minutes of the sounds of someone moving around the room, then a drawer opening and a chair scraping.

"Get Ledderer! Now! This is an emergency!"

"Mumble."

"Karpov! Get him! Now!"

About three minutes of room noises.

"Mumble mumble."

"Listen, General! You'll have to call Sanchez off of the two flunkies! They laughed in Todd's face! Todd's worried because their only link is Sanchez and Pwester had dumped him before any of this came up!"

"Mumble ... would tell you any ... to get them ... stupid...! You made a damned ... Screwups like ... them dead. ... me in it! Mumble."

"Listen, you stupid jerk! If you have them killed it'll make the evidence they already have reliable!"

"Mumble mumble ... vidence because they don't...."

"You think you're safe? Well, they put Sanchez on some sort of machine. A lie detector! They know a hell of a lot more than you can guess!"

"Mumble mumble ... ell me what.... I'll have your ass you...! Mumble!"

"You have anyone killed, you stupid ass, and I'll guarantee that you're right in the middle of it! You've already proved you don't have the intelligence to pull it off! None of your plans seem to work! It's all fallen apart and all you want to do is cover your own worthless ass!"

"Mumble mumble."

"That did it! You (A string of vile epithets that Todd thought might melt the machine) idiot! The Kraut is right about one thing there! We're all committing treason against our race! I'll see you fry in hell, you (Another round of profanity)!"

There was a CLACK!, sounds of movement, then a door slamming loudly. There wasn't anything else except for the clicks and such on the rest of the tape.

"How long before they turned it off?" Todd asked.

"They didn't. They put in a new tape when I got this one," Gretta said.

"Then he left the room?" Todd asked. "Where did he go?"

Carl took the interphone to ask security to find Karpov, then they waited again. The com buzzed and Carl answered, said "uh-huh" a couple of times, grunted and said, "Seal it!" and hung up.

"Karpov is sitting at his office desk with a recorder in his hand," he said. "He's dead. Mike says it smells like cyanide in the room."

"Get that recorder in here! Fast!" Gretta shot at him. "Seal his room, too. Don't trust anyone but Mike."

Carl picked up the com and spoke.

Again, they waited. After a few minutes Mike came in to hand the tape recorder to Gretta, who told him to search the office and Karpov's rooms thoroughly, photographing every detail. He went out and she placed the recorder on the table, ran the tape back and punched the play button.

"Please deliver this to the hand of President Krause. Do not listen to it first, as it is most personal.

"Please use print so these words are most clear. I suspect there is a listening device in the room."

Gretta attached the recorder to the printer and started it.

Madame President, I wish to confess that I have become a thing, not a person. You spoke of traitors to their race, and I must say I am become exactly that. I am the bad link here.

I want nothing more than to tell you who is the head of all this, but I must protect my family. I will say no more than that there is a plot afoot to overthrow the government. The senate is RIDDLED with spies and worse. The military is backing the coup all the way. They want the Space Service under their control again. They wish a war with Goombridge. There is a great DEAL of money to be made from that ARMING.

The real head of this is not NOW in the military, but leads them. They are being LED along a GENERAL path in a sense, but are fully aware of what they do. MORE THAN LED! Much more! One could call it `the most unkindest cut,' if one likes Shakespeare.

I digress and ramble, trying to procrastinate.

See that my family is well taken care of. They are innocent of any wrongdoing.

Forgive me. I make no excuses. I am badly flawed, and I have caused enough pain to enough people. I cannot, must not, continue in this vein.

I am sorry.

I now am taking a capsule of cyanide. Goodbye.

"A listening device?" Carl said. "In his office?"

"And other places," Todd agreed. "There was more than that in having this printed. He stressed certain things with the capitals for good reason. Bring all this tape to my scoutship. There are no devices there!"

They went to the ship.

"We can safely discuss this here," Todd said. "You can see he capitalized `riddled' to tell us to look for a hidden meaning. He then capitalized the word `led' and quoted Shakespeare. Led plus more led is ledder and plus even more, in Shakespearean vernacular, would be Ledderer. Not in a general way.

"Ex-General Ledderer, who makes a lot of money from dealing arms. I think he really feared for his family and has tried to tell you who it was without endangering any of them. Get them some protection as fast as you can.

"We know who's behind it, but have to move fast. We have to avoid problems. We must avoid a lot of bloodshed. We have to root out everyone in the senate who's in on this. That's by far the most important point for the moment.

"What can we do about Ledderer?"

"We have to get absolute proof, which means we have to make Sanchez blab," Tab said. "I say we can handle it pretty well once the public is convinced. They'll handle the military."

"We'll do that," Todd agreed. "Exactly how we threatened to do it before. We'll have you and Kim make a sharp focus for the anti-asteroid laser, then let them know we won't hesitate to leave dry ashes where they dare to march against the president!

"I've got a military mind to that extent. They're a bunch of traitors and mutineers – and worse – and are therefore at war with the legitimately established government. I won't pause. I'll shoot them down before they make three steps!"

Tab shook his head. "Grow up, Kid! It may come to

something like that, but it's our job to try to avoid it," he argued.

Todd grinned his sheepish grin. "I do act a lot like a kid sometimes, don't I?" he said. "Gretta, can you trace the contacts of the senators lately? Anyone who's had too much contact with Karpov."

"Hmmm. Kirsch, too," Tab said. "And don't forget General D'Angona. We know he's in it up to his neck. Find any politicians who have contact with him. Him and Kirsch both is too much for coincidence and we all know it. Get Mike to set up personal security for you and Carl. It could get hairy!"

"You be careful, too," Gretta said. "They'll probably try to assassinate me, now, but they've already tried to kill you."

"Too true," Tab said. "Let's get this started. Battle stations everyone!"

"Battle stations!" Pwester ordered. "Keep in touch!"

Todd and Tab watched as Gretta and Carl met Mike and went back inside, then they headed for Luna Base and intrigue in their own quarter.

Chapter ten

Ella met them as they came into the tunnel to say that Col. Sanchez had an accident and was dead. His air supply duct from the recycler had jammed shut during the night when a brace had dropped on the tensioner and snapped the separator solenoid shut.

"How convenient!" Todd snarled. "Of course, the safety spring was jammed by the same brace bar."

"My! How did you *ever* guess!?" Ella said sarcastically. "You must be psychic! It is such a freak accident for a brace to fall from a strut arm, bounce thirty one feet sideways and four feet three inches upward, twist *just so* and end up in a slot only half an inch wider than it is!

"Didn't they used to give a big cigar for that?"

"And it just *happened* to fall after Sanchez had taken a strong sedative to help him sleep because the tension of being under investigation had given him insomnia!" Todd cried. *"That* must be why he didn't hear the warning buzzer when the carbon dioxide built to a dangerous level! What a *coincidence*!"

"We haven't checked for sedatives yet, but I don't doubt it," Ella agreed. "Is it a setback?"

"It plays right into our hands," Tab said. "Ledderer's main source of information from Luna Base is gone now. He's panicked. Karpov was right to call him a stupid ... what he called him."

"I heard something about that. He had a heart attack at the vacation palace?" Ella asked.

"In a way," Tab replied. "You can say his heart was attacked by cyanide. Self-administered."

"You don't mean that Karpov was in this mess!!?" Ella exclaimed. "Good lord! I thought he was one of the few we could trust. I thought his name was dropped to throw us off!

I really did!"

"I can't understand you people!" Todd cried. "Gretta, and now you! We *knew* he was in it before we ever went to Earth!"

Tab laughed and said, "He was very suave and charming. Women would always try to refuse to believe anything bad about him."

Ella glared and started to say something, but Tab continued, "Just the same way you or I would refuse to believe anything bad about Gloria Stellarz. She's so beautiful and sweet and so pure and innocent and vulnerable. If you can believe the things her directors and fellow actors say she's a total vicious bitch in reality."

Todd grinned at her. It was true. People went more by appearance than by facts. He would watch himself and what he accepted about any others – be sure it was more than `a feeling' that they were all right.

"We still are in a position where I can see a choice among a small war, a coup, a revolution, selective assassinations – give me some ideas!" he pleaded.

"I got an idea I could use a meal and a shower," Tab said. "Let's meet in S six (Security offices) in an hour, say?"

They all agreed. Todd would speak with Kim and could listen to whatever he had gathered since they left. He wanted some food, too.

Kim had his telltale with him on the table where he could watch the indicator lights, Ella had her bag with its various devices, Todd had his briefcase with its little secrets and Tab had his coded recorder. They spent more than three hours going over each tiniest detail and making a chronological list with information from them all.

"Lossiter was in the mess with several people, Meier was over in Luna R&R with others and we know damned well Sanchez didn't do it himself, so we have at least one more operative here," Kim said slowly, staring into space. "I have security lists and had a lot of people checked out. Most of them don't realize they key a recorder every time they use a card on a door."

"How long would it take you to call up where everyone went for the past two weeks?" Ella asked.

Todd pulled the computer screen around.

"Patch the ship's security into Luna Base," he said to Kim.

"It only reads what the ship inputs," Kim said.

"It also asks questions and requests further data, which means it's hooked into the general system, which means it can be read," Todd said. "I know these machines. I've worked with them while the system was developing.

"When the machines were being installed on Luna I was under the tutelage of one Old Mike Cogsworth, who designed certain features into them."

Kim grinned and set up a coded sequence which had the ship interface with the base system. "Full modem and cross-interface two-way data draw is the most complete access I can get," he said.

"That's the easy part," Todd said. "I have to remember the pattern for all this. It's a matter of ... I think I have it. Let's see."

He worked for a few minutes until the "Error" signal came on, then punched "Query ?" and waited.

Data Access Error #35. Insufficient Data Input. Format and Reschedule.

When Tab saw the #35 he grinned and leaned back. "I take it that error thirty five in any sequence is your code key?" he said.

"Thirty five accesses secondary coded channels if the correct code sequence is followed," Todd replied, punching in a few additional characters."

Denied.

"Damn it!" Todd exclaimed, and again called up the "Error

#35" sign. It was the fourth try before he got the "?" he was waiting for.

"I see how this works now," Tab said. "The machine doesn't understand the question so you somehow reprogram it."

Todd nodded and quickly typed in: *Program Incomplete. Substitute Order Security >A< to > Printer Only. Reprogram From < Drive 2.*

There was a short pause, then: *Dive 2 Not Responding.*

"Warning! System Flaw! Copy Records This Section on > Printer Disk for Computer Access Only! Warning! System Flaw! There is an error on disk! Override System ~E~! Todd printed.

A red light flashed for twenty seconds, the screen rolled, went blank and came back on with a sign, "Instructions, Please?"

Todd removed the printer disk and inserted another one after running a strong magnet across it, then printed: *Confirm Data.*

Warning! Disk Damaged! Data may be lost! came across the screen.

Sim-Flaw Repaired: Systems Test: Cmplt. Return To Normal Operation. Todd typed.

"Okay, you have a disk with everything you want, but it's computer-access only," Kim said. "How do you get around that?"

"The `computer access only' is a security measure," Todd said. "It's generally stored in the computer's memory, but can be put on a disk with a signal for emergency repairs, then is copied back into the machine's memory and the disk automatically erased. The computer itself won't release any of that information except to an operator with the code. We don't have that code and we don't want anyone to know we have this information or they might run or otherwise cover their tracks.

"I just made the computer `think' there was a systems

emergency and had it save the data on the closest disk, which was this printer. The disk in the printer is already programmed to print whatever is on that disk. The orders here aren't the orders of the base computers and, indeed, this printer has no coded program *not* to print anything!

"I then input that it was a simulation test so the comps won't record the test took place except to give time and ST number, which isn't recoverable in this system.

"Kim will now thank the base computer and disconnect the modem line."

Kim did.

Todd removed the unformatted disk in the printer drive and reinserted the disk with the information from the base computer. He quickly set the machine to print all the data on the disk.

"This will take an hour or so so let's get some cool refreshment while we're waiting," Todd suggested. "I'll key the door for my admittance only, though I'm sure there's no one on my ship who can't be trusted totally."

They went to the mess room where they talked with a few of the crew for awhile, then returned to S6. There were four hundred and ninety four sheets of paper covered with data.

"Our only real problem here is because we can't ask our computers to sort this for us. We have to do it by hand," Todd complained. "The forelist identifies everyone by their code number. There are seven hundred plus numbers for the people and two hundred twenty nine destinations. The personnel numbers start with PLB and a three number series, a hyphen and another three number series.

"Use the last three and record the number and its destination number, date and time. I'll take oh oh one to two hundred, Ella gets two oh one to four hundred, Kim gets four oh one to six hundred, and Tab gets six oh one up.

"Use voice on your personal recorders. We'll input it all into our computer security system to have it sorted and such by the computer. We could scan it, make a disk, and have the comps sort, but that would leave 'way too much information cluttering up the backup recorders, so we'll have to trudge through.

"I'll say something like this."

Todd picked up the first sheet, turned on his recorder and said, "Oh nine three, R twelve, five seven, oh seven thirty six. Data. One seven seven, M two, five seven, oh seven thirty six."

He turned the recorder off and asked, "Got it?"

They all said yes and moved to the corners of the room with individual stacks of the paper. It took six hours twenty minutes to read all of it into their recorders, then they called up the security console. Todd placed his hands on the reader and his eyes to the biscopehead. It recorded his finger and palm prints and his retinal prints. Only he could ever use the information in the system under that identification.

"I'll bet there's no way around that!" Kim said.

"How much?" Todd asked. "If it can be put in it can be gotten out. It may not be easy, but I'll bet I could do it."

"No bet!" Kim replied. "I learned my lesson with that base computer!"

Todd took each person's disk from the recorder to input it into the computer on one file, then told the computer to sort the data with oh oh one, oh oh two and proceed numerically until all data was sorted.

They again waited. Soon, the machine said all data was sorted and stored. Todd took that disk, labeled it, then put it in his briefcase.

"Gonna print it?" Kim asked.

"It won't print," Todd answered. "I don't have the glitches in this system we put in the others. Nothing with a special security classification would be copied onto a disk with ANY information already on it. The printing program must already be on the disk before the information. There's probably an easy way to get information off of this disk, but we haven't discovered it yet."

He then placed a new disk and told the machine to list all information as to when oh oh one met with others chronologically and to proceed numerically through the list. He had to tell the machine it would assume a meeting whenever destinations matched.

"Wait!" Tab said. "Why not do a simple chronological listing where everyone is placed at all times, then pull our numbers for Sanchez, Lossiter, and Meier, have them listed from that and eliminate fifty percent of it?"

"I see what you mean," Todd said. "I want any and all other suggestions."

"Why not list the destinations chronologically, excepting mess and their work stations?" Kim suggested. "Then you can pull destinations where our three were involved."

"We can do that all at once," Todd agreed. "That's good.

"Anything else?"

No one said anything, so he punched in the request and had it put on the screen after it was recorded onto the disk.

"Looks promising," Ella said. "Can you have this one printed out?

"Add number three oh five. That one seems to have spent an inordinate amount of time with Meier."

"Probably a boyfriend, but we'll do it. It catches the eye rather quickly," Todd agreed. "Four nineteen catches my eye.

"Anybody else?"

"Oh six two," Kim said.

"Five twelve and three seventeen," Tab added.

Todd punched the codes in and they waited until the printer stopped chattering.

"We have about twenty pages there," Kim said. "I suggest that Todd read a page, note on his own recorder anything that catches his attention, then he hands the page to me, where I'll do the same, then to Ella, then to Tab. We can then input all of that into the computer and will have four separate view-points. Nobody discusses anything with anybody else. We won't have outside influence."

They agreed that would be best. It took more than an hour. They were careful.

They brought the disks to Todd, who put it into the computer.

"This part is the main trouble with counter-espionage and detective work," Tab said, yawning heavily. "In the books they bounce from adventure to adventure, fly all over space, crash their scouts at near light speed, but crawl out unharmed, shoot each other up – it never stops.

"We've just spent ten or twelve of the most boring hours of my life reading stupid code lists! My head aches and my back hurts! I haven't been able to crash a single solitary scout, I haven't shot anybody or been shot at! If this is as exciting as it gets I'd rather be a librarian! At least I could read about adventure and excitement!"

They all laughed and agreed. They were exhausted.

Todd finished his instructions to the computer and the printer chattered for a couple of minutes. There were four full pages of printouts. Todd picked them up to compare them. Tab was sitting with his feet on the table, Kim was drinking his umpteenth cup of coffee and Ella was looking over his shoulder.

Todd placed the first and third sheets together, typed the two items that caught his eye, added several more, then typed some more instructions. The printer chattered and spat out about three quarters of a page. Ella read it over Todd's shoulder and nodded. Tab raised one eyebrow. Kim laid his head to the side and waited.

"There it is!" Todd said.

There were a number of things on the list that pointed unmistakably in one direction as to guilt while at the same time pointing very strongly to where one may place his trust.

Todd needed no pointing finger for trust on "The First Attempt". He knew each member of the crew very well and knew that none of them could be involved in this kind of intrigue. His problem was more one of how to act so his mission could be accomplished on Luna Base before any interference from the military was possible.

Tab had taken his scout and a copy of some of the strongest damaging evidence and was off to find the "Ecstasy". They would rendezvous in fixed orbit above Earth if all went right while Todd and his crew would make their move on Luna Base at the same time.

Captain Grovich would have three people with him and Captain Neels would have three with her. They would round up four people apiece and would force them into "The First Attempt" while Todd, Ella and Kim would round up the six more important traitors.

Timing was everything at this point. This could become a very treacherous exercise if anything at all went wrong. Luna Base could be secured solidly and all possibility of further sabotage eliminated, leaving only the group on Earth itself to round up. The "Ecstasy" and Tab must see that the military was prevented from taking action. Tab must see that the president and Pwester were safe.

Everyone was ready. It would take one communication from Tab to start the ball rolling. There must be no least hesitation. The whole thing must be done suddenly and surely. The lists had pinpointed the fact that a certain small group of people met at the times when something was happening and the ones they had known to be in the conspiracy were always among the group. There had been fifteen on Luna Base, but Sanchez was dead. Todd hoped one or more of them would cave in under close questioning and would implicate Ledderer directly.

This was timed so they would know where everyone was. It was toward the end of the rest period they called night in the

Luna Complex where there was a slight chance they could handle this quietly enough to where the other personnel would never know about it until it was over and done with.

The message came. Tab had patched to the satellites, but would remain silent unless and until there was response from Earth. The greatest hope was that no one would have to know the ship was there.

Tab reported that Captain Lopez, Todd's old crewmate, was handling the minor details while Natalie was handling all communications and strategy.

"I'm outside and headed for the island," Tab announced. "Go!"

Todd snapped his fingers and they ran from the ship to their assignments. They met no resistance until they were all back on the ship except Grovich and his crew, but no one would dare to challenge him. The Base Security tried to stop them, but Grovich called that they were on assignment from the president herself and security was to check with "The First Attempt".

Todd had returned with his prisoners. He said the operation was almost finished and the president had ordered the operation due to the sabotage that had been done there. The head security officer used the red line to the president, who stated she had indeed given special assignment to Commander Todd and his orders were to be followed to the letter. The operation was to remain as confidential as possible.

Gretta didn't know at that time what Todd was doing, but she was a fast thinker. She knew Tab had called from the pad on the island, had told her to get her most trusted guards, to secure herself and Carl in the private quarters in the palace until he got there. He would explain at that time, so she knew it was big.

She drew up a decree on her recorder of internal security,

which she could act independently on until the senate was in session, giving Todd the authority to conduct investigations into sabotage, espionage and treason in the highest places. He had complete authority and answered only to her. He took orders from no one but her until such time as the security council met to debate the options. That would take months. This would be over in hours, she was sure. She was slightly worried in that Todd was too much the patriot and tended to be impractical. He felt the ends could be made to justify the means and that was a dangerous psychological trait.

Well, Tab could hold him back.

But Tab was here!

Then it must be settled to Tab's insistence. Todd had no idea how much he relied on the older officer's opinions and how much he listened to the reason from both him and that Ella character – and character she was! Gretta couldn't help but feel a strong fondness for the outspoken Colonel Ella Forbes!

The die, as the saying goes, was cast.

She took the printout from the machine, affixed her signature, then entered it into the records, putting the time back to a few minutes after the close of the working day. That was as far as wouldn't be entered in the permanent record until the morning.

Now she must wait. Carl and Tab came in and she poured them coffee.

"Tell me about it, Tab," she ordered. "All of it!"

"We used the computers to tell us who on Luna Base was behind this coup so we decided to round them up," Tab explained. "Don't ask me how Todd got that information from Luna Base's security computer. That stuff's supposed to be impossible!"

"Cogsworth and Todd coded in a number thirty five override sequence," Carl said. "There's not much about a computer Todd can't get around."

"We know all about that," Gretta said. "Todd tried to

explain how to use it, but we neither one ever understood it."

"Todd screwed it up four times before he got it right," Tab said. "Anyhow, we decided to wait until sleep time on Luna Base. I would bring the "Ecstasy" here and then would land to protect you, though I doubt anything will happen here. No one will know unless we missed somebody – and I really do doubt that, too!"

"I see," Gretta said. "The "Ecstasy" will defy the military on the planet if they try any cute tricks. Same argument Todd gave them at the senate riots."

"Right," Tab replied.

"Let's go to your ship," Carl said. "Take us to "The First Attempt"."

"Why?" Tab asked.

"I want to face those saboteurs and I have a strange feeling about this place. I do *not* think this is a good place for the president to be right now."

Gretta protested, but they were soon en route to the moon. Tab moved the scoutship directly into the port and aboard the mother ship, then had the ship sealed before he would allow Pwester or Krause out. He then led them to room S6 where Todd and Kim were questioning Lossiter. Todd was surprised to see them.

"Where's Colonel Forbes?" Carl demanded.

"In her infirmary treating some bruises where one of these garbage-bags resisted arrest," Kim answered.

"Tell her to come in here and to bring sodium pentothal in large doses," Carl ordered.

"We can't use truth serum!" Todd cried.

"Why not?" Pwester asked. "We're aboard a Space Survey ship where standard laws are suspended. I'm senior officer here so I make the law! I say we use the pentothal! Now, Captain!"

"That stuff can kill you!" Lossiter cried.

"I'm supposed to be concerned for your worthless life?" Carl said. "You tried to assassinate my top pilots and destroy nine billion dollars worth of scout ships and you think I'm going to bleed over what happens to your ass?

"I hope you do croak as soon as the pentothal drains every little thing you know!"

"I demand a lawyer!" Lossiter yelled.

"You're aboard a stellar class Space Services ship!" Pwester snapped. "You don't get any damned lawyer, no judge and no jury! I'm the law here! If I tell Commander Todd to gut shoot you with a heat laser he will gut shoot you with a heat laser! Is that clear?"

Lossiter was sweating profusely. "No! You can't do that!" he whined. "It's inhuman!"

"And you're human?" Pwester sneered. "A ... slimy thing ... who would sell out his own race for a buck? You, I'm supposed to treat with respect and dignity?

"You're getting me damned close to actually using a heat laser to get information! Pentothal is too good for your type!"

Todd was about to protest. Tab caught his eye and shook his head.

"I never did anything to you!" Lossiter whined. "You got no right to treat a Terran citizen like this!"

"I got the right to do anything I want while on this ship!" Pwester snapped. "And you're a traitor to every Terran citizen alive today! If you again claim humanity or rights as a citizen I'll have you shot on the spot!"

He was yelling and working himself into a rage.

"Captain Grovich!" he ordered. "Give me your sidearm!"

Grovich nervously handed Pwester his laser.

"I'll shoot you down like the vermin you are! You lousy damned scumball!" Pwester yelled in his face. "By God, you give me an excuse! Any excuse at all! I'll start at your worthless feet and work up with this thing! You stinking slime!

"I'm going to ask you a question or two and I had damned

well better like the answers I get! By God, I'd better like the hell out of the answers or, by God, I'll fry you a little at the time!

"Now! You tell me about this crap! All of it! We know about Kirsch and Karpov and Ledderer and that bunch so if you lie I'll know it in a picosecond! I won't give you a second chance you stinking slimy lousy damned second-rate excuse for vermin!"

Todd suddenly noticed that, though Pwester was now screaming and jumping up and down and waving the laser under Lossiter's nose his eyes were hard and calculating. He wasn't in the least red in the face.

So! He could relax! Gretta and Tab had seen what he was doing from the start. Grovich was looking pleadingly at him and, as Lossiter couldn't see him, he winked at Grovich, who then slowly grinned.

"You'd best start right at the first and tell us all of it," Gretta said. "We know most of it and basically only want to be absolutely sure we don't miss anyone who would start a war that could destroy Earth just to have a little power or to make a few dollars.

"I'll consider cooperation from any individual when time comes for sentencing. You will every one be tried for treason and only the president can commute that sentence. Think about that!"

She went out into the hallway. Todd followed her. Ella was rushing up with her bag. Todd explained what had happened and suggested she go on in and lay out a row of syringes on the table for psychological effect.

"If they think we can get the information no matter what they do they'll be more inclined to try to save their own skins by telling all of it," Gretta explained.

"Why, what a dirty stinking trick!" Ella said. "Threatening the poor, scared traitor that way! I'll bring charges right to the World Presidential Palace door!"

"There's no one at home right now, Dear," Gretta said. "Come back when you can stay longer! Maybe I'll be there next year!"

Ella winked and went into the room.

Two hours later Todd and Gretta were summoned back to the room from where they were sitting in the mess room chatting with the crew. Lossiter was led out and locked in the section with the other prisoners, but isolated in a separate room.

"He couldn't talk enough," Tab said. "I suppose all of them will be like that. They have no honor and are basically cowards. They'll do anything to save their own worthless skins. He was number three under Sanchez and Meier. He knew a lot of the main contacts on Earth and had some strong suspicions of who the `control' was at Luna Base.

"It seems there was one person no one knew who kept tabs on everyone else for Ledderer – who has better sense than to trust any of this trash. I've sent Grovich and Neels to get her.

"We know the basic line of command in the military."

Kim suddenly stood and went to the interphone, then announced that the "Ecstasy" wanted to talk to Tab. They went to the com shack where Natalie reported a contingent had moved against the palace and surrounded it. She wanted to know if they should now go onto the satellite hookup.

"Wait!" Tab said. "Get the hookup ready. We'll be there in a few minutes. Be ready to fry HQ one A twelve. Focus right on it!"

They hurried to Tab's scout and Todd, Tab, Gretta and Carl were soon aboard the "Ecstasy". They planned what they would do on the way. Gretta moved quickly and directly in front of the cameras, nodded and began: "People of Terra!" she announced. "There is an attempted coup at the vacation palace at this moment led by the saboteurs you have heard mentioned on your newscasts lately.

"We know of this and are not there. General D'Angona and his people are directing the palace coup attempt from HQ one A twelve. Commander, destroy that building! Now!"

Lopez fired the beam cannon at sharp focus. The building and a small area around it were turned to vapors.

Gretta continued.

"I warn all others involved in this scheme to run! We know who you are! The military troops near the palace area will withdraw immediately or will be destroyed. I have a list of officers who will be tried for treason against the people of Terra. I have a complete list of politicians and their aides who will likewise be stood against a wall and shot upon conviction, some of whom are right at this moment at the palace. Your coup has failed! Run, rats! Run!"

She turned to Todd to ask if that was enough. He agreed it was exactly what the situation called for.

"The next step is to begin rounding up the biggest shots. Work from the top down," Pwester said. "We know who we can trust on Earth.

"I want Ledderer to face me as his prosecutor on sabotage and treason charges!"

They spent several days directing the operations on Earth from the ships in orbit. The moon was secure. "The First Attempt" was orbited directly opposite the "Ecstasy", the world in between.

No one could find Ledderer.

Chapter eleven

The hard thing was to trace it all back again. Six days of computer search and sitting around making lists. They had to find where Ledderer had gone. His munitions plants had been seized on evidence. Now information from many years back must be checked. There was a hideout somewhere that had been prepared as much as fourteen years past. It was, to say the very least, tedious.

For the first time in a long while Todd thought of the short encounter with the alien, Truncd. Here was precisely why Terra wasn't to be allowed into the family of worlds. They would never be allowed. Even now, in this day and age someone like Ledderer could exist and hundreds of others such as Karpov and Meier and D'Angona would follow them. They would betray their entire race.

Todd quite literally wanted to put his face on the desk and cry like a lost baby. He couldn't blame the empire. They had thousands of worlds to think of, to protect.

Would Earth ever change?

Yes, it would slowly change. Maybe they could avoid actual quarantine. That was one hope he could cling to.

He also thought such an immensely long few days ago that maybe he could make a difference.

Arrogant fool! That had really blown up in his face! If the aliens had some form of observing them, and he was sure they had, they must really think Earth people are something! That's what happens when you get too sure of your own importance. Life will slap the arrogance out of you!

Todd sighed and went back to reading his lists. Ella came over to say, "You can quit any time you like. I've found as much as we're likely to find."

"What'cha got?" Todd asked.

"Low grav tiedown furniture not on present inventories and

never disposed of, large supplies and varieties of preserved, frozen and canned foods and water, not on present inventories and never disposed of. A neat little ship that was in for too many repairs while the repair shops had purchased too many long-distance parts, little things like that," she replied.

"Out-system?" he asked.

"Not enough for that. One of the moons of Jupiter or Saturn or even Neptune. Maybe an asteroid setter?" she said.

"I don't see it. Maybe Ganymede," Tab said, coming to them. "He won't get too far from communications and you flatly well know he intends to return after things die down a bit."

"We can use the Mantas to search," Todd said. "They have the detectors that will show where he is. He can't escape.

"I'll take Jupiter, you take Saturn and we'll meet back on Deimos."

"Fair enough," Tab said. "Anything for a little action!"

"Ain't it the truth!" Ella said. "Another day of this and I'll need therapy!"

They took off and did a survey scan of all the moons, then met at Deimos.

"No way," Tab complained. "He's not there. I think he never left Earth, myself."

"Let's look Pluto over," Todd said. "I'm sorry, but I fully disagree. He isn't on Earth because almost anyone who sees him will tear him limb from limb.

"Maybe the asteroids?"

"Not in the asteroids," Tab said. "Your girlfriend surveyed them on her way out. No energy use there at all that doesn't pinpoint as standard stations."

"Crap! I'm sure he couldn't survive Pluto, either!" Todd said in exasperation. It's just ... just...!" he broke out laughing.

"What?" Tab asked.

"Where would you go to hide in millions of square miles of unused territory in light gravity where you wouldn't be very detectable and could remain in communication?" Todd asked.

Tab raised the eyebrow.

"Look up," Todd suggested. "We're orbiting around the obvious. It would be the easiest thing you can think of to get down here undetected – particularly if you've established a routine.

"We both know he's established a routine."

Tab groaned. Todd shrugged and made a sick grin.

This meant using the computer readouts here to trace. It took four days and then they only had an area to search. There were a good many people on Mars where there were domes being built that would house an entire city and farmland area, but the area where they had an indication was pretty desolate. It was, as was much of Mars, a very large and deep valley with sharp, high mountains all around. There was a large wide extinct river in the bottom where water could be found if one dug a ways, but the minerals in the water made it most difficult to use. The metal salts made it hard to find any that could be used directly for irrigation. Distilling it out there was expensive, so most brought their own water. The power plants near the domes use their excess heat to distill water for the cities, but nuclear plants produce a lot of excess heat while the fuel cells used in the out areas do not.

"How are we going to do this?" Tab asked.

"I really don't know," Todd replied. "I guess we land and find some kind of guide or something."

They left Tab's scoutship on Deimos and went aground in "Final Exam". They immediately found the people were more open and friendly than they would have believed and would do anything they could to help – they had heard of the trouble on Earth. They certainly didn't want the military to ever get strong again, but they simply didn't have any time to act as guides. They were a pioneer society and each had his duties.

The politicians were chosen by rotation vote. Nobody wanted the jobs so it had been necessary to set up a system that would make politics a requirement for all qualified.

The two spacers spent the full day and night inside the small temporary dome, which was simply a half-sphere of a balloon two kilometers across and half a kilometer high with an airlock every couple of hundred meters. It was filled with air to set it up, then it was ready to go. Plants were then brought in for food and air replenishment and portable tent-like individual housing units, flexible hoses for water and sewage.

It was an amazing place with amazing people that soon found Todd feeling much better about the race. He knew exactly where he would retire if they would have him! He could deduce from the attention Tab paid to each detail and the way he studied what they were planning that soon Tab would decide to stay here, too, but he would stick around for a few more years. There was no sense in denying he needed Tab and that Tab knew it.

Would Natalie be willing to make a home here? That was a very important part of any decision.

"We can take a surface skimmer and go where we please," Tab said, breaking his reverie. "We have to supply fuel. They have none to spare, but the auxiliaries from the "Exam" will fit the plug-ins nicely. I told them we would leave an extra fuel cell in rental for the skimmer."

"There isn't enough air for a skimmer out there! Come on!" Todd cried.

"It skims by taking in fine sand, charging it electrically and discharging it through some kind of setup," Tab refuted. "Mass/action/reaction still works nicely. We can encircle the planet in two days. The things move very fast, but the fuel cell will only last three and a half days at full discharge. Where we are going is six hours away so we shouldn't have any trouble. We'll carry food, water and a few instruments and things.

"Ready?"

"Let's get the show moving," Todd agreed.

"I'm bringing along a few little items that should prove very interesting in this kind of place. Primitive things from Earth," Tab said, taking a long bag to hang from his shoulder. "Stuff my father gave me."

They found the strange vehicle, which was a platform with a large clear plastic bubble on it and a weird mass of tubes and fins underneath, to be really efficient. The air supply was on the rear portion of the platform and was well-protected. Tab and Todd were both expert natural pilots and this was a very easy vehicle to operate. So long as one didn't fly directly into a mountain it seemed very safe.

They waited in the valley for night, then found their quarry the easy way – with standard infra-red scanners.

"He's got the ship in a cave to the left of the dome," Todd said. "The dome's against the base of the mountain and is under an overhang. It's a fortress. We can't get in there.

"You said when this started you never got shot at. I'd say that's about to change – dramatically!"

"You sure go to extremes," Tab said, grinning. "He's made one big mistake. He's sacrificed visibility for safety."

Tab took out his pocket computer and figured for a few minutes.

"Should do it," he finally decided. "Our only real problem will be keeping the ship there. This rock isn't too hard so maybe we can cause a cave-in."

"I doubt it," Todd said. "How do we get into that dome? It's too well-protected and is silvered so a laser's useless."

"This is a different world. It isn't that big on technology so I won't be, either. I can get them out of the dome. I just don't want them to be able to run on me," Tab argued. "See that ledge over there? We have to get to it."

"That's around five kilometers or so from the dome and a kilometer above it!" Todd protested.

"I know! Let's go," Tab said.

They were on the ledge an hour later. The skimmer could

climb any angle less than ninety degrees in this slight gravity – and they were out of sight of the dome until they were almost to the ledge. They put the skimmer back out of sight and went in their suits to the edge. Tab brought a strange device Todd recognized as an old weapon called a projectile rifle .30-.30 from pictures.

Of course! A laser beam would be reflected from the dome, but a projectile would puncture it! The air would begin to leak, then they'd have to get out and to the ship! The calculations were of trajectories figured from the gravity, the distance and the.... What was it called? Some kind of velocity?

Tab placed the rifle carefully on a rock and used a level to get the angle exactly right.

"I have to figure without air resistance, but this should do it," Tab said. "I'm used to firing it. The noise won't be bad here because of so little air."

He carefully squeezed the trigger and Todd heard a distinct little "pop" sound as fire shot from the end of the rifle. He kept the binoculars trained carefully on the dome.

The top of the dome jerked slightly, but that was all.

"Got it!" Tab said happily.

"But it didn't do anything!" Todd cried.

"What did you expect? A gaping hole you can walk through from a bullet smaller than your little finger?" Tab asked. "I'll put a few more little holes in it. They'll seal them I suppose, but I can put more in it."

He took the rifle up and fired six more times in rapid-fire sequence, then grabbed the binoculars. He suddenly jumped and yelled, "Wooo! Look at that!" and handed Todd the strong binoculars.

The airlock was flapping and the dome was collapsing. Two people were desperately trying to put masks on.

"I hit the retainer bar on the damned door!" Tab cried wildly. "I could have shot a thousand times if I'd tried to do that and it wouldn't've work!

"But where's Ledderer? He isn't one of those two!"

The two had struggled into the oxygen masks as a short fat figure came to the door trying to put on a mask. He was waving and signaling to the other two, but they turned to run for the ship.

"I'll be damned!" Tab said. "They're going to run off and leave him there! That's Ledderer!"

"Yeah. He's fallen down," Todd said. "What's the matter with him?"

Tab studied the scene a moment, then handed the binoculars to Todd. There obviously wasn't any oxygen in the cylinder Ledderer grabbed.

"Either of the others could come back and they could share oxygen to the ship," Tab answered. "They're going to let him lay there and die!"

"That's what he would do to them so why should they be any different?" Todd said. "Such a lovely class of people, these traitors. I think they will have made a fatal mistake by not saving him ... yes! Look!"

The two were now running from the cave back toward Ledderer, but it was too late. He wasn't moving and the two stood arguing, they looked along the valley.

"The ship's keyed to Ledderer, the same way our scouts are keyed to us," Tab explained. "There's no way he would trust them. Now they're stuck.

"Wait!"

He watched as the two went back to the cave to drag out a skimmer.

"Come on!" Tab yelled. "Dive directly at them! They'll get out of the valley and we won't be able to catch them! They know the area! We don't! We can't even identify them!"

Todd jumped into the little skimmer while Tab stayed outside with the rifle. The radios in the suits worked well through the bubble and Tab explained he would try to hit something on their skimmer that would disable it.

They came down the mountain at sickening speed as the others started up the valley. The traitors saw the skimmer coming and suddenly opened their own up.

"I have to figure trajectory," Tab said. "Don't try to catch them, just match their speed and run as steady as you can. I'll shoot for the fuel cell."

There was a flash from the rifle, then another, then another.

"Try to get closer," Tab ordered. "They...."

There was a tremendous explosion on the skimmer ahead and pieces of debris rained all around them.

"What the hell!?" Tab yelled.

"You hit the oxygen cylinder by the fuel cell and you hit the fuel cell," Todd said. "The hood over it held the oxygen – the hydrogen mixed, they changed gears or something and there was a spark."

"I forgot about the hydrogen fuel cells!" Tab cried. "My God! I must have hit it first shot! I didn't hit any oxygen cylinder. The hydrogen cell is half in and half out so it leaked directly into the bubble. They were in the center of a bomb!"

"Let's go back and check on Ledderer," Todd said. "Then home. You got shot at and we made a chase, albeit not in a lightspeed ship.

"I'm tired of this!"

Chapter twelve

The trip back to the big dome was slow and dismal, pulling what was left of a mangled sandsled with Ledderer's and his two henchmen's bodies. They would have used one of Todd's tricks to get into and to operate Ledderer's ship but had no three-D camera with them. Todd said with the camera he could have made pictures of Ledderer's eyes for the retinal prints and pictures of his hands through a pane of clear glass for the other prints and made the ship turn over control to one of them.

The people on Mars didn't appreciate the fact the three were brought in dead and suggested it might have been better to leave them where they died. The necessary inquiry now would waste time they didn't have.

Todd called Carl on Earth, who immediately sent back a total responsibility acceptance claim from the president herself, thus relieving anyone on Mars from having to take any steps. Ledderer was a wanted criminal on Earth.

Todd and Tab spent three days on Mars using as an excuse the necessity of gaining other evidence against Ledderer. Tab filed a future claim for some land, as did Tab. They would be next door neighbors, a mere six kilometers apart. They must take possession of the land within ten years, which meant Todd would be thirty four when he retired. He seriously hoped the Space Services would be fully operational on their own by then.

He was more and more convinced that, should they be able to make Mars and independent colony – and he and Tab could well help with that! – it would be accepted by the Empire even if Earth never was.

Perhaps in his own lifetime he would be able to meet face-to-face with the aliens. Perhaps he would be able to invite Truncd himself (Itself? Herself?) to spend some time in his private home on his large ranch.

Dreams! All silly children's dreams! Truncd had described himself as a nine foot tall Tyrannosaurus rex! What would you offer to a large reptile for food or entertainment? What were their customs? Their morals? Were they carnivores? Herbivores? Omnivores? Something else?

Still, his dreams had very often brought him what he wanted. Perhaps, just perhaps....

Should he tell Tab about the encounter? He could very well trust his friend to keep silent about it.

He spent a few hours beating around the bush, then told Tab all about it – how he and Kim had decided to keep quiet, and why. Tab agreed and said that, quite frankly, he had never seen any qualities among the Terran races that would make it desirable to others to meet them. He had seen some evidence in his scouting that there were others and that those others could easily contact them. He wasn't in the least surprised they hadn't.

He was worried to a slight extent about the nuclear things. The only uses on Mars was power generation and there was nothing said against that, but all those bombs on Earth!

"I wish we could drop them all on the neutron moon!" Tab said sadly. "That would be best for the human race, the Goombridgians and the universe, for that matter. I'm sure that if we got rid of ours they would get rid of theirs.

"This silly, childish `You first!' attitude is dangerous."

When they returned to "The First Attempt" with the bodies and evidence (Gretta had given the ship and all other possessions of Ledderer on Mars to the Martians) and were en route back to Luna Base, the exhaustion they had been postponing hit them. Inside the system they must travel on STL (Slower than light, which was true no matter what else isn't, but that's a very complicated bit of science and even concerns dimensional transference) it took them nineteen hours to reach Luna. Both Tab and Todd slept the whole trip.

Being in the lowered gravity of Mars and being curious and excited most of the time they simply weren't aware of their bodies' requirements. Ella lectured them about their health as though they were little naughty boys.

There was turmoil on Earth. Seven people in the senate and many more aides and clerks were shown to be part of the overthrow attempt. The people of Earth were demanding a complete ongoing investigation of all public officials that would be far beyond the abilities of all investigative agencies combined.

Carl Pwester, being somewhat the cynic anyhow, suggested they simply release the names and addresses of any known to have been in it. The mood of the people would save the cost of the trials and executions. The people would tear them apart.

Maybe the people of Earth were finally fed up enough with what these kinds of manipulators had done to see they never again got any power.

Todd was skeptical. They would again become corrupt and would again try to gain personal power. That was deeply ingrained in the human race – some of them.

The military was now the basic problem. They would throw the Goombridgian situation in the peoples' faces in an attempt to scare them into preserving the forces. Carl's cynicism wouldn't help anything there and it was far the best thing that he hold his tongue.

Would Gretta be able to handle that? Certainly she would be unable to stop them altogether, but could she defang them to any realistic extent?

Wait. Maybe he and Tab could put in a word or two in the right places. Mars must be supported all the way. They were the real hope of the Terran Empire, such as it was.

Tell Gretta about the encounter with the alien?

In ten years when he retired and she was no longer president.

What a mess! But it was a tiny bit better than last year and, hopefully, it would be even a little better the following year.

Ella came to inform him they were down and in the Luna Base hangar. Natalie had left some messages, which he read. They were mostly a report of the project in protecting against the military and a personal note to look for a nice piece of real estate on Mars, preferably on a lake.

He grinned. She had been to Mars on a training mission so knew he would fall in love with the place. It was her way of telling him she would be glad to spend the years there with him.

After retirement.

There was a message to call Gretta on the secure channel on a matter that was moderately important, but not critical. He went to the comshack (Why call it a shack? Where did that come from? It was just a large room in the ship!) to place the call on the coder. The coder placed the voice in digital and put it among a lot of noise where the decoder on the other end would select the proper bits by mathematical formula and put it back together properly.

"Gretta? You had something for me?" he asked.

"Todd, we've found the military has stockpiled more than a thousand nuclear warheads on Titan four," she replied. "They had no authorization, so you can go in and get them. They're supposed to be hidden, but I've given Kim the coordinate points. I don't know what to tell you to do with them. Just get rid of them. Drop them into the sun. Anything."

"We'll handle that," Todd said. "How are you going to handle the military thing?"

"Be totally honest. Tell the people it was the military mind that would have seized the government in an attempt to perpetuate itself," she answered. "We'll have to keep a force, but they're to be better controlled.

"I have to do it, Todd. To move too fast there would spell disaster if only because a great many people believe the stupid Goombridge Fairy Tale.

"What did you think of Mars?"

"I intend to retire there," Todd replied honestly. "I filed a claim. They're a wonderful society that could teach Earth a lot!"

"They're going to inflate the new big dome in a few days and will make a sports and entertainment complex in the one they're using now," she said. "They're a pioneering society and are much different from us, but there's no way to work the system here. They're apolitical while we have too many special interests here, most of which are silly and are only out to make something for themselves by taking something from everyone else.

"What does Natalie say about Mars?"

He was silent for a short moment. How come everyone in the whole damned galaxy could see what was between him and Natalie when they had hardly even had the time for a single kiss?

"Todd?"

"Oh, I was daydreaming again," Todd said. "She wants a place there. On a lake."

Gretta laughed. They said their goodbyes, then Todd called Kim to get the coordinates for the warheads on Titan 4. The asteroid was easy enough to get into and out of so he called Tab. They decided to go after the warheads and drop them into the sun as Gretta had suggested.

They returned to Luna Base three E-days later, then went on a survey. Carl had to caution Todd that the presence of "The First Attempt" in solar space was too much a symbol so it would be better if they were to leave for a time.

That was fair enough.

Todd used a lot of the four months they spent on the survey to grow up a bit. He was now 24 years old and, though he was the youngest commander in the history of the Space Services (A record that only his great granddaughter would ever equal), he was still much too juvenile in some ways. The influence of Tab, who was 36, was inestimable in that period and their friendship steadily grew stronger. They were to spend most of the rest of their lives highly dependent on one another – Tab being the solid rock and Todd being the impetuous one.

Todd also settled down philosophically. He was barely able to avoid becoming a cynic like Carl while dropping away some of his idealistic ideas. All-in-all he became more pragmatic while still holding on to his idealistic dreams, which was to say he would always dream those dreams, but would be able to accept that it wasn't reasonable to think he could have them all or even a large majority of them.

They found a dying red sun with ice planets set, as Natalie had said, like jewels in a black velvet case. The system was far enough away from others that he and Carl took the red sun while the others took a single scout to a system that proved to not have any planets.

One of the planets had a civilization under the ice, frozen forever, to be seen only by instruments. There were castles and port slums and all the medieval trappings down there.

"I wonder what the people were like?" Todd asked. "Were they reptiles, like Truncd? Were they mammals? What were their dreams? Did they look at the stars and want to go?"

"Hmmm. According to the readings the sun died rather suddenly," Tab said. "It was too small to be stable and something happened to put out the fire so to speak. It didn't explode and become a red dwarf, it simply died.

"I wonder if they were a good race who would expand into the galaxy or one like Truncd mentioned who would destroy themselves with internal conflict? Were they like us – a race who could go either way?

"We'll never really know unless your empire has records. This sun died almost a billion years ago. I doubt that any empire has been around for that long."

"If they were reptiles they might still be alive down there. Frozen into perfect suspension," Todd said. "There's a satellite. It's broadcasting a steady pulse of energy."

"I noticed," Tab said. "I found one other system with that sort of satellite."

"You did?!" Todd exclaimed. "I never heard of it!"

"It was an "X" planet," Tab explained. "I decided to let them remain in peace. They were a living society."

Todd thought for a moment, then stated, "The rules say that should we find a primitive society we will designate it "X". It doesn't say anywhere I've read that they must be alive. As you say, let them rest in peace."

He entered "Four planets cold and dead, no obvious value. One planet primitive society, early iron age. Planet designated "X" with no reason to enter other planets. Recommend whole system be designated "X". Passed unanimously. Commander Robert Cole Todd, SS."

"Passed unanimously?" Tab said, grinning.

"You agree and I agree," Todd pointed out. "We're the only ones here. That automatically makes it unanimous – right?"

Tab slapped him on the back and laughed. "How do you diagram without sensor pictures?" he asked.

"Ever hear of computer enhancement?" Todd asked. "I take the laser-reflective readouts, add color, remove the ice and, Voila! See?"

Pictures of a pastoral scene with a castle and blurry cattle or something in a field and rows of what looked like corn plants with sunflower blooms appeared. He "printed" the scene on tape and labeled it with the planet's number.

"One castle proves our point," Todd said.

They then went back to "The First Attempt", where they shared what they had done with the other pilots and with Ella and Kim.

"We ARE the panel, so your unanimous vote is certainly true!" Ella said. "It's rather sad they died like that. I wonder what they would be now if their sun hadn't burned out?"

"Either extinct.... Probably extinct," Tab said. "I don't see any society enduring a billion years. Not even ten percent that long."

"You mean we will die out in only a hundred million years?!" Ella cried, innocently. "Oh my! Are we ready for it?"

"Remind me to bring it up at our next executive meeting so we can make evacuation plans," Kim quipped. "We can form a study group who may recommend a committee to investigate and report to an oversight board who will decide whether to present it for our consideration. That should take about that much time.

"I think funding of a million dollars a year to be disbursed through my offices?"

"Careful!" Ella challenged. "I'll tell them about your pink teddy bear!"

Todd could see him wondering if he dared take things any further. A coup attempt and all that intrigue and adventure was only a few days behind them and here they were, back to normal.

Robert Cole Todd, Admiral SS, Rtd, made his way through the mob. His son, grandson and granddaughter were trying their best to keep up with his long strides. He was well-known here on Mars and was well-respected. The people would make way for him.

He approached the group at the center of attention and reached out to touch the huge "nine foot Tyrannosaurus rex" standing there beside what looked like a man's body with an elephant's head. He knew that was the being known as an Inktan, but his real interest was the Feach. The terrifying creature turned to stare at him.

"Yes?" it asked.

"Are you called Truncd?" Todd asked.

There was a hissing laugh, then, "No. Truncd is at Hospital to deliver a group to Taint where there is a plague to be stopped.

"You have met her?

"I did not know there had been contact before except for the Inktan professor, Rimalt."

"We spoke once a great distance from here on the radio," Todd replied.

His heart almost stopped when the huge being reached down to lift his three year old granddaughter, Natalie, and to place her astride the wonderful strange creature known as a Zulian. Natalie squealed with delight as the Zulian humped off down the road with several other children on its back.

The Zulian was a white tube with horny plates at four places on its bottom that it used as feet. It would plant the front two, hump up like an inchworm, place the rear two close to the front, plant them, lift the front and straighten out the tubelike body, moving about six feet per hump. Todd knew that, for some reason, the Zulians were the most respected and loved beings in the galaxy.

The sleek black-furred Zeenan and a big hairy Vendan were speaking with Tab a few meters ahead as Todd thanked the Feach, then moved to talk with the tall Kheth for a moment. The Kheth were reptiles who looked almost human except that they had no hair.

A Swaz, who are amphibians, and an Acnian, who are almost as hard to classify as the Zulians, came to speak with the Kheth, then the group moved away.

The Acnian had compound eyes. Todd understood they were what is called T-hynotics and could hypnotize him with a glance. No one in the Maitan Empire would misuse such a talent.

As of today, Mars was a member in good standing of the Maitan empire!

Earth was probationary and may not make it, but *Mars was in the empire*!

Todd had discovered the empire wasn't a political thing, that peoples from the entire galaxy were members because it gave them contact and trade with one another. All the empire was in reality was a huge trading guild. There were the machines and such to give legal opinions, but no one had to take their advice – except on one or two very important points: One did not make *any* contact with a developing world or in any way interfere with it. Period. No argument allowed. There were no explosive nuclear devices allowed. Period. No argument allowed. The nuclears were simply too dirty and there were literally billions of planets in the galaxy that did *not* have life in any stages, so it was asking very little indeed that they leave the ones with life alone.

Earth had been strongly warned about that! The military had become relatively strong for awhile and had begun the same old Goombridgian war talk again. They had put outposts on some near planets. Now the empire people had moved in to clean up the mess – for good this time. They had immediately taken Tau Ceti 4 into their empire, then had come to Mars to offer trade.

Goombridge and Earth were both on probation. They could enter the empire in as little as twenty seven or so years (25 Maitan Galactic Standard years), but only if they didn't again start the old hostilities or war talk with each other or with anyone else.

The Inktan, Rimalt, had made it very plain: "There are more than three thousand trading members of the Maitan Empire. None of whom are at war with anyone.

"Tell me, why should we allow you to be the exception?"

That strange funny little being called a Mentan, the Emperor's Ambassador that everyone on Earth had fallen in love with (except for the military idiots who had almost murdered it), said much the same. It said it in funny and biting ways, addressing the senate and supreme court and making fools out of them. It had literally shown that every one of those people were perjurers because they took an oath of office to uphold the constitution, then did everything in their power to destroy its power.

They took an oath, they were lying when they took that oath, lying under oath is perjury, they are perjurers.

Finally the people of Earth would stick together to try to rid themselves of their worst flaws.

It would happen now.

Todd had lived to see his dreams come true. He had married Natalie, he had then come to live on Mars after establishing a career almost as great as that of Mike Cogsworth, he had landed his own ship on worlds where no man had ever stepped foot, he had met the aliens from the empire, had spoken with them, had reached out his hand and had actually touched them! He had progeny, a fine son and grandson and a granddaughter who was this moment screaming her glee while humping down the road on the back of an amazing alien creature.

His grandson was there above the crowd sitting on the shoulder of a "nine foot Tyrannosaurus rex" – a Feach scientist who was, incidentally, known as one of the finest medical researchers in the entire galaxy!

Who was it – Robert Cole Todd, student – who once said that one man couldn't really make a difference?

C. D. Moulton's works are available on most major outlets as printed or e-books. CD writes the CD Grimes, PI mysteries, the Det. Lt. Nick Storie mysteries, the Clint Faraday mysteries, the Flight of the Maita science fiction series, books on orchid culture and many others of many types. Mystery, adventure, intrigue, science fiction, fantasy, paranormal, mild erotica, and factual.